"Come On, Jack, Let's Not Make More Of This Than It Is. Old Habits Die Hard."

"Old habits die hard?" Bitterness tinged his voice. "And here I thought this was consolation sex. How many excuses do you think you need to sleep with me?"

"You think these are excuses to sleep with you? They're reasons not to get involved with you again."

The absolute conviction of her words stung. "I don't recall asking you to get involved."

"Oh, no," she scoffed. "That would be way too much commitment for you. You haven't changed one bit."

"No. I haven't changed. And neither has this attraction between us. All I want is for you to admit it."

* * *

Don't miss the exclusive in-book short story by *USA TODAY* bestselling author Maureen Child after the last page of *Tempted Into the Tycoon's Trap*.

Dear Reader,

I can't tell you how much fun I had writing this book. Not only was it an honor to match up with so many great writers for the Hudson continuity, but I just loved writing about this powerful Hollywood family.

I've long been fascinated by the movie industry. (Finally, my fifteen-year subscription to *Entertainment Weekly* paid off!) I adore the glitz and glamour of Hollywood's golden age almost as much as I enjoy the gossip and scandal of modern moviemaking. Add in a spunky, smart-aleck of a heroine and a hero who hides his darker side behind a charming facade and you've got a book that was just darn fun to write.

Please check my Web site for news, contests and information about future books, www.EmilyMcKay.com.

Emily McKay

TEMPTED INTO THE TYCOON'S TRAP

EMILY McKAY

Silhouette

Desire

Published by Silhouette Books

America's Publisher of Contemporary Romance

Special thanks and acknowledgment
to Emily McKay for her contribution to
The Hudsons of Beverly Hills miniseries.

To my grandmother, Hope Eleanor Gaskill Gray Caton,
the matriarch of my own family, who has a lot in common
with Lillian Hudson, not in particulars, but in spirit.

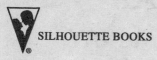 **SILHOUETTE BOOKS**

Recycling programs
for this product may
not exist in your area.

ISBN-13: 978-0-373-76922-3
ISBN-10: 0-373-76922-9

TEMPTED INTO THE TYCOON'S TRAP

Visit Silhouette Books at www.eHarlequin.com

Printed in U.S.A.

Books by Emily McKay

Silhouette Desire

Surrogate and Wife #1710
Baby on the Billionaire's Doorstep #1866
Baby Benefits #1902
Tempted Into the Tycoon's Trap #1922

EMILY McKAY

has been reading romance novels since she was eleven years old. Her first Harlequin Romance book came free in a box of Hefty garbage bags. She has been reading and loving romance novels ever since. She lives in Texas with her husband, her newborn daughter and too many pets. Her books have been finalists for RWA's Golden Heart Award, the Write Touch Readers' Award and the Gayle Wilson Award of Excellence. Her debut novel, *Baby Be Mine,* was a RITA® Award finalist for Best First Book and Best Short Contemporary. To learn more visit her Web site at www.EmilyMcKay.com.

THE HUDSONS OF BEVERLY HILLS

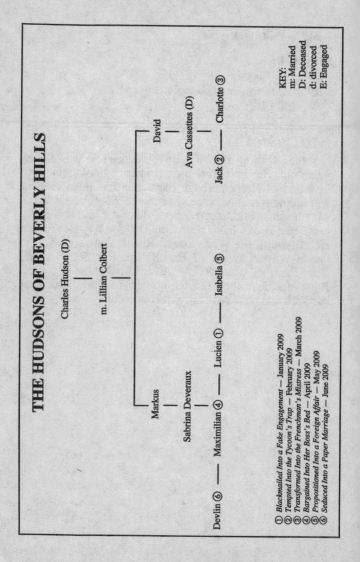

Charles Hudson (D)

|
m. Lillian Colbert

Markus — David

Sabrina Deveraux — Lucien ① — Isabella ⑤ — Ava Cassettes (D)

Devlin ⑥ — Maximilian ④ — Jack ② — Charlotte ③

① *Blackmailed Into a Fake Engagement* — January 2009
② *Tempted Into the Tycoon's Trap* — February 2009
③ *Transformed Into the Frenchman's Mistress* — March 2009
④ *Bargained Into Her Boss's Bed* — April 2009
⑤ *Propositioned Into a Foreign Affair* — May 2009
⑥ *Seduced Into a Paper Marriage* — June 2009

KEY:
m: Married
D: Deceased
d: divorced
E: Engaged

Prologue

If his cousins Dev, Max and Luc Hudson could see him now, he'd never live it down. When Jack Hudson glanced at the woman beside him, he almost didn't care.

Cece Cassidy slouched in her chair, feet propped on the back of the seat in front of her, a barrel of popcorn wedged between her knees.

"I can't believe you're eating that," he said to her.

She glanced at him from under her lashes. "I can't believe you're not gonna try it. The Crest has the best popcorn in L.A." She gestured emphatically toward the bucket. "I mean, this is real, hand-popped corn."

To illustrate her point, she shoveled another mouthful in, then closed her eyes in apparent ecstasy. His pulse skyrocketed.

Petite and curvy, Cece had a face that was pleasing without

being beautiful—or maybe beautiful without being pretty, he could never quite decide. She had an odd little bump on her nose that came from her father's Italian ancestors. Her eyes were wide and a little slanted. Her mouth was full and lush— the one trait she'd gotten from her mother. She wasn't tall, gorgeous or dumb. In short, she wasn't his type, which may have explained why he wanted her so badly.

Whatever the cause, his current attraction was completely unexpected. Cece was his grandmother's goddaughter. They'd practically grown up together. Yet, when he'd run into her last month at the Hudsons' annual Valentine's Day party, he'd been instantly attracted. He'd been fighting it ever since, despite the fact that Cece seemed determined to drag him all over L.A. to whatever famous landmark she found interesting.

She was a sweet kid. At twenty-four, she seemed impossibly young, even though she was only three years younger than he. And then there was the fact that she was Lillian's goddaughter. That nearly everyone in the Hudson family adored her. If he slept with her, he'd probably end up breaking her innocent little heart. Then the family would collectively lynch him—just what he needed.

Giving in to one temptation—since he couldn't give in to the other—he grabbed a handful of popcorn. "Remind me again why we're here."

"First off, this is a great old theater."

He glanced around the restored 1940s-era movie theater: plush seats, purple carpets, hand-painted murals. It was beautiful. "They don't make them like this anymore," he agreed, then added, "I think the screening room at Hudson Manor has a bigger screen."

She grinned. "Exactly. Which brings me to point number two. You don't ever go to the movies." He raised an eyebrow, but before he could protest, she continued, "I know, Mr.

My-Family-Owns-a-Studio. You see plenty of movies. But you don't go to the movies. This—" she gestured to the audience "—is a completely different experience than what you're used to."

He managed to pry his gaze from her animated face to glance around at the crowd that had turned out for this midnight showing. A Jedi Knight and a Wookiee sat two seats down. He had to admit, they were certainly enthusiastic.

Cece raised her pointer to gesture. "And finally, this is the best sequel ever made." He must have looked doubtful, because she cupped her hands over her mouth and dropped her voice. "'Luke, I am your father.' Come on, that's great stuff."

She paused, obviously waiting for him to crack a smile. Given his complicated relationship with his own father, one might assume he'd find solace in the redemptive story arc of Luke and Darth Vader. But the truth was, he'd never bought it. In his experience, men who were jerks were always jerks—especially those who abandoned their kids to pursue their own goals.

Rather than say all that aloud, he threw out, *"The Godfather II—"*

"Nope, not even close. This has the great cliffhanger ending, plus the yummy romance between Princess Leia and Han Solo."

He looked at her, surprised. "Really? I would have pegged you for a *When Harry Met Sally* fan."

"Nah." She waved a hand. "Give me sarcastic Han Solo over sentimental Harry any day."

"Shh!" The Jedi Knight growled at them.

Jack ignored the guy and leaned a little closer to Cece. The butter from the popcorn made her lips gleam in the flickering light of the movie previews. Her shoulder brushed his as she reached for more popcorn and he felt the familiar spark of heat—something she seemed completely unaware of.

Sparring over pop culture aside, he wanted more from her

than this. He didn't want a movie-going buddy. He wanted her. Naked. In his bed. Tonight.

"Tell me something, Cece." She dragged her attention away from the movie screen to look at him just as the setup text began to scroll. "What are we doing here?"

She pointed to the screen, looking at him as if he was crazy. "*Empire Strikes Back,* remember?"

"No. What are *we* doing here?"

She smiled, but it wasn't her usual cheerful grin. She looked a little sad, actually. Head cocked to the side, she said, "When we met at the party, you just seemed a little lonely. Like you needed a friend."

Maybe it was his innate irritation with her movie choice. Or maybe it was his resentment over being called *lonely.* Whatever. He was tired of waiting.

He grasped her chin and tilted it up before pressing his mouth to hers. She tasted of butter and salt, and when he kissed her, there was a moment when she didn't move at all. Then she rose up to meet his kiss, her tongue darting against his. Heat rocketed through him, making him instantly go hard.

He pulled back, searching her expression. "Cece, I don't need a friend."

Her eyes were wide and it seemed to take her a minute for his words to sink in. Then she nodded, licking her lips as if she were afraid of missing a bit of his kiss.

"Let's get out of here," he suggested. She stood so quickly her bucket of popcorn showered the floor.

Four months later—just as he'd predicted—he broke her heart.

One

So, Lillian Hudson wanted Hudson Pictures to make a biopic about the legendary World War II romance between her and her husband, Charles.

From the moment Jack Hudson heard her announcement during the annual Valentine's Day bash at Hudson Manor, he knew trouble was brewing. The week before, he'd stopped by for a visit and found his grandmother watching *The Wave*, which Cece had written. At the time, the image of the Statue of Liberty disappearing beneath a hundred-and-fifty-foot tsunami seemed particularly foreboding. Now he knew why.

Undoubtedly, Lillian was going to hit him up to convince Cece to write the script for *Honor*, which would be hard for him to do, since Cece wasn't speaking to him.

He was clutching a crystal champagne flute when Lillian made the announcement. He'd downed the nearly two-hundred-dollar-a-bottle Dom Pérignon, ditched the glass and had been making his way toward the bar ever since. He skirted the bustling dance floor, dodging waiters bearing trays of more champagne, fervently gesticulating directors and dewy-eyed starlets.

Any minute now, Lillian would corner him, and he wanted to have a glass of Patrón in his hand when she did. Unfortunately, he was too slow. He'd almost reached the open bar when he heard his grandmother's voice behind him.

"You don't seem pleased about my announcement."

He turned to face her. Despite her age, Lillian held herself with the same graceful elegance that had made her a legend on the silver screen. She wore a long, sparkling gown, no doubt designed to show off the diamond necklace shimmering around her neck. Her crystalline blue eyes held a spark of humor, as if she knew why he'd been avoiding her.

"Naturally, I'm thrilled, Grandmother." She held out her arms, so he leaned forward and gave her a buss on the cheek. "I think your love story will make a brilliant movie."

"Charles always thought so. One person or another has been batting around the idea for years. But when Charles died, I didn't have the heart to do it without him."

For a moment his normally vibrant grandmother sounded so sad and frail, he almost didn't voice his concerns. "I'm glad we're doing it now. But you said you want the movie released on the studio's sixtieth anniversary. What's the rush? There's no hurry, we should take our time. Do it right."

The illusion of Lillian's fragility vanished. "When should we do it, my boy? For the seventy-fifth anniversary? For the hundredth?" She didn't wait for him to answer her rhetorical question. "No, I've made up my mind. If we don't do it now, it may never get done."

Since he could see there was no point in arguing with her, he shrugged. "Then I assume you'll be wanting me to hire a screenwriter."

She smiled gamely. Still an attractive woman at eighty-nine, age had done little to dim her charms. "Ah, my boy, you know me too well."

He continued before she could say more. "First thing Monday morning, I'll talk to Robert Rodat." He paused to gesture for a drink from the bartender, who must have worked at past parties because he automatically handed Jack a Patrón. "He worked with Spielberg on *Saving Private Ryan*."

Lillian waved her hand regally. "No, no. That won't do at all. The last thing I want is someone who's done another World War II drama. The story of how your grandfather and I met and fell in love is special. We need someone who will bring a unique approach to the project. Someone with a personal touch."

Her eyes glittered with the same cunning he remembered all too well from his childhood. After his mother's death, Lillian and Charles had raised him. As a result, she could see right through him.

She raised a hand to toy with the diamonds at her neck. "No, I have the perfect screenwriter already in mind."

Just what he was afraid of.

"You remember my goddaughter, Cheryl Cassidy?"

Cece? How could he forget her? With her quick wit and lightning-fast sense of humor. With her lush full lips and warm brown eyes. With her sable hair that spread over his pillow like a curtain of silk.

"Naturally, I remember her."

He couldn't possibly forget Cece. As Lillian and Charles's goddaughter, she'd been a near-constant feature at Hudson Manor during his youth. When they'd met again three years ago, he'd found she'd blossomed from the pesky kid who used to follow him around into an irresistible woman.

In short, he'd never forget their brief but passionate affair. Or how badly it had ended.

"Well," Lillian continued, seemingly unaware of his train of thought, "we haven't seen nearly enough of dear Cece lately."

"No, we haven't." Probably because she'd been avoiding all of the Hudsons since he went and broke her heart. She'd even stopped coming to the Hudson parties. Undoubtedly one of the reasons he found this party so dull.

"I believe she'd be perfect for the job. She has a strong connection to the family. She'll do the project justice. Besides, I understand she's quite talented. I believe her previous projects have done well."

Little Cece had grown into a firecracker not only in bed, but in the industry as well. She was quickly becoming known for the kind of witty, fast-paced scripts that audiences loved. One of the industry rags had recently described her as the David Mamet of adventure movies.

"Her previous projects have grossed a combined two hundred million dollars," he stated drolly.

"Exactly. So why isn't she working for Hudson Pictures?" Lillian tapped a finger on his arm in a gentle reprimand. "Why isn't she making those millions for us? This project is the perfect opportunity to bring her back into the fold."

"Frankly, I'm not sure this is her kind of project."

"Nonsense. As a child she used to love listening to Charles talk about the war. She's practically family."

"Grandmother—" He tried one last protest, but she quickly cut him off.

"I won't be swayed on this, Jonathan."

He smiled wryly. "You must be serious indeed if you're resorting to calling me by my given name."

"I am. First thing tomorrow I want you to visit Cece. If anyone can convince her to do the project, you can. I'm counting on you."

As she turned and strutted away, he gave a little half bow.

Something about his grandmother had always inspired that kind of formality.

So the edict had been issued. It was his job to bring Cece back into the fold. What Lillian didn't know was that it was Jack's affair with her that had driven her away in the first place.

Cece Cassidy stared at the blinking cursor on her computer screen, biting back an expletive of frustration. Her son, Theo, sat on her office floor babbling nonsense to himself as he flipped through the pages of one of his books. Though just shy of two, he was verbally precocious. If she cursed aloud, within minutes he'd be running through the house chanting her verbal mistake.

"Curses," she muttered aloud.

"Curses," he chimed.

She chuckled, despite the fact that the third act of her latest script had fallen flat. She picked up a cinnamon Altoid from the tin on her desk and popped it in her mouth, considering her dilemma. The bad guy had been vanquished, the bomb defused, the hero had saved the day. "What am I missing?"

Theo looked up from his book. "Brown bear, brown bear."

"Nope, that's not it."

Holding her fingers poised over the keyboard, she waited for inspiration to strike. Thank goodness the doorbell rang.

She hopped from her chair. "Ah! A reprieve."

Yes, she could have let the nanny get it, but that wouldn't offer the kind of diversion she was looking for. She caught up with Maria in the entrance hall. "I'll get it, Maria. You go watch Theo."

Maria looked relieved. Though she was Theo's full-time nanny, in truth she had little to do, since Cece worked from home and kept him with her much of the time.

A moment later, Cece yanked open her front door, ready

to hug whoever had saved her from having to face her slimy bad guy and her limp third act. Then she saw Jack Hudson on her porch. With his shoulder wedged against the support column and his hands tucked into his jeans pockets, he looked completely relaxed. As if showing up on the doorstep of her tiny Santa Barbara cottage were an everyday occurrence. As if the last time he'd seen her, he hadn't broken her heart.

Squeezing tight to the doorknob, she braced herself against a wave of emotion and shock. The floor seemed to tilt under her feet, making her feel light-headed and woozy.

Except for the year she'd spent in France, she'd lived in California her whole life and weathered countless earthquakes. None of them shook her like the sight of Jack standing on her doorstep.

"Can I come in?"

Panic clawed its way through her gut as she considered his request. Surely, if he knew the truth—if he'd discovered her secret—he wouldn't be here politely asking to come in.

Feigning a cavalier indifference she didn't come anywhere close to feeling, she bumped up her chin, quirked an eyebrow and blocked his entrance with her body.

"Well, well, well. If it isn't Jack Hudson. The villain of my life's story." It should be illegal for former lovers to show up unannounced on your doorstep. At the very least they deserved foreboding theme music, like the shark from *Jaws*.

His gaze was shuttered and impenetrable. "Don't be overly dramatic, Cece."

"I once destroyed the entire Eastern Seaboard in a tsunami. Trust me, I know when drama is called for."

And at the moment, she felt how she'd imagined her characters feeling just moments before they'd been swept away by a tower of water: terrified and helpless. Jack had the ability to destroy her completely. He just didn't know it. She hoped.

"Are you going to let me in or not?"

"Not, I think. I have nothing to say to you."

The lie was so blatant she half expected an act of God— one of her tsunamis, perhaps?—to wipe her out on the spot, taking all of Santa Barbara with her.

The truth was, she had a great deal she should say to him. Most of it involved her son, who was innocently playing in her office just a few thin walls away. Not just her son, *their* son.

She'd spent every day for the past two and a half years dreading the moment Jack Hudson showed up on her doorstep, demanding answers about the child she'd supposedly "adopted" while abroad just after breaking up with him.

Swallowing her growing fear, she considered her options: let him in and face the music? Lock the door and call her lawyer? Run like hell?

"This isn't personal," he said.

She studied his face. Not a flicker of interest. None of the heat with which he used to gaze at her. None of the smoldering passion that had lit his eyes back when she'd known his body as well as her own. But Jack had always been an expert at hiding his emotions.

However, what she didn't see was the spark of anger that would indicate he'd discovered her secret. It made her bold.

"Not personal, huh?" she scoffed. "I almost even believe you."

It was pure bravado, though. Inside her pulse was racing. If he hadn't guessed the truth, she wasn't going to let him linger around to see Theo with his own eyes.

She stepped back into the house, ready to shut the door in his face, but his words stopped her.

"Lillian sent me."

Cece's heart leaped into her throat. The drive from Jack's house in Malibu out to her little cottage was a long one. If

Lillian were ill, it might warrant Jack making such a drive. "She's okay?"

"She's fine. But she misses you."

Relief and nostalgia washed over Cece. Lillian had always been one of her favorite people in the whole world. And it had been so long since she'd seen her.

It was the price she'd paid. When she'd decided not to tell Jack about Theo, she had to cut the Hudsons out of her life forever. Still she missed Lillian dearly.

Jack must have sensed her hesitation, because he edged forward, bracing a hand on the door frame. His nearness seemed to suck all the air out of her lungs. His eyes traced the lines of her face, making her wish she'd known he was coming. Then she could have prepared her defenses against him. Or at least put on makeup.

As it was, her face was scrubbed clean, her hair still damp from the shower she'd taken after her morning jog. She wore her oldest jeans and her lucky T-shirt—a ratty Led Zeppelin concert T she'd swiped from her father's closet a good fifteen years ago.

Jack was dressed simply in jeans and a crisp, cream linen shirt, which accented his tan. He looked absurdly good. Frankly, it was ridiculous that anyone could look that fresh and appealing.

But Jack—well, all the Hudsons, really—had always had that quality to him. With his chiseled jaw, perfect cheekbones and firm lips, he could have just as easily worked in front of the camera as behind it.

"Let me come in so we can talk. After all we've been through together, shouldn't you at least hear what I have to say? Don't you owe me at least that much?"

She felt a pang of regret so strong it literally rocked her back on her feet. He had no idea just how much she owed him.

So she stepped back and let him enter. As she led Jack

down the entrance hall toward the living room at the back of the house, she was painfully aware that Theo and Maria were just around the corner in her office. If Jack heard the faint murmur of their voices, he didn't comment. For her part, she was all too aware of them and could only hope Maria had enough sense to keep Theo occupied.

Jack didn't insult her intelligence with the pretense of small talk as they walked. She returned the favor by not offering him coffee or water. They were well past those sorts of pleasantries.

When they reached the living room, she plopped down onto her favorite leather club chair, tucking her feet up under her to keep from fidgeting and revealing just how nervous she was. Not that that kept her from toying with the single strand of hair that had come loose from her damp ponytail.

"So what is it Lillian wanted? I assume she didn't send you to invite me for Thanksgiving dinner."

He quirked a sardonic eyebrow. "It's a little early in the year for that."

"She does like to plan ahead."

"Saturday night, at the Valentine's Day bash, Lillian announced she wants us to make a movie about how she and Charles met during World War II."

Charles had worked undercover for the OSS in France during the occupation. While in Marseilles, he'd been bewitched by a cabaret singer, Lillian, only to suspect she was collaborating with the Nazis. Lillian had been working as a spy for the French resistance. Despite the war, despite the danger and mistrust, they'd fallen in love. And their love had lasted a lifetime. After the war, Charles had brought his bride back to the States where together they'd made movies showcasing Lillian's talents. Those movies and their love formed the foundation for Hudson Studios.

Trying to calm her nerves, Cece figure-eighted the strand of hair through her fingers. "Makes sense. It's a great story. Action, romance, tons of drama and suspense. Kind of like *Atonement* meets *Casablanca*. But with a happy ending. It'll make you millions. Probably hundreds of them."

"She wants you to write the script."

She stilled. *"Me?"*

"Yeah. I was as surprised as you are."

"I don't do those kinds of scripts."

"That's what I told her."

"I write action-adventure movies."

"I know."

"Evil geniuses trying to take over the world," she continued. "Natural disasters. Ticking time bombs. That kind of thing."

"Absolutely."

"And I *don't* do love stories."

She could only hope she didn't sound too emphatic.

However, she must have given herself away because Jack shot her an appraising look. "You've turned into quite the cynic."

She rolled her eyes. "You got cynical from that one comment?"

"Your tone said a lot. I hope I'm not—"

"Don't flatter yourself. Trust me, I've always been this cynical about romance. My parents had one of the rockiest, on-again, off-again relationships in the history of Hollywood. I was contemptuous of love when I was still in diapers. Which is exactly why I'm the last person who should write a script about Lillian and Charles."

Jack lowered himself into the chair opposite her and leaned forward, propping his elbows on his knees. "But she's convinced you're the only one who can do her story justice."

Unable to contain herself, Cece hopped up from her chair and began pacing. "That's ridiculous."

But was it?

Moviemaking was in her blood. Her father, Martin Cassidy, was one of the greatest directors of all time. Her mother, Kate Thomas, had been one of the seventies' sex-kitten starlets. The image of her legendarily long legs and tousled blond tresses had graced countless movie posters and the bedroom walls of teenage boys.

Unfortunately, Cece had inherited none of her mother's good looks, but rather her father's coloring, height and prominent Italian nose. Which went well with her love of pasta and tiramisu, but resulted in her being all of five foot four and possessing curves and features that were…well, somewhat ego-deflating for the daughter of one of America's iconic sex symbols.

Her disappointing looks had made for tough teenage years. Lots of "helpful" adults had told her allegories about ugly ducklings. By twenty she'd accepted she was never going to blossom into a swan, but made a damn good sarcastic duck. Which lent itself naturally to her screenwriting ambitions.

However, nothing in her repertoire had prepared her for a job like this one. This story didn't need rapid-fire pacing or witty dialogue. No, it required something far trickier to pull off. Emotional honesty. Vulnerability. Was she ready for that?

Still, as a kid, Cece had watched dailies instead of *Sesame Street*. Her parents had told her movie pitches instead of bedtime stories. Stories were a part of who she was at the molecular level.

No story more so than that of Lillian and Charles. Even today, as Cece thought about their relationship, a thrill of excitement shot through her. Their love was the stuff of legends. Of childhood fantasies. Well, of her childhood fantasies, anyway.

Jack, too, had been woven into the fabric of her childhood imagination. She'd spent a lot of time at Hudson Manor as a kid. Long summer days and endless weekends following him around the grounds, begging him to play hide-and-seek with her. Or, once he was too old for such games, climbing trees, watching the clouds drift by, dreaming of the grand romance and adventure they'd someday share.

And look how that had turned out. No grand adventure. No lasting romance. Just heartache, betrayal and regret.

Resolutely she shook her head. "No. I can't do it."

"You mean you won't do it."

"Fine. Can't. Won't. Whatever. The point is, it's a bad idea. I don't have the chops to tell that kind of story."

Jack flashed her one of those sly half smiles of his. "Come on, Cece. You could write the transcripts from C-SPAN into an interesting movie."

She let herself feel only a twinge of pleasure at his compliment before squashing the emotion. "Besides, didn't I once swear I'd never work for Hudson Pictures?"

He leaned back, stretching his arm across the back of the sofa. "Sure. But that was just after we broke up, when you were a little more emotionally invested in loathing me."

"Good point." And now if she held to her promise, she'd all but be admitting she was still emotionally invested in him. Cunning jerk.

He must have sensed her hesitation because he pressed forward. "You know this is a story you'd love to tell. This is a story you've been itching to tell since you were a kid." He pinned her with a blue gaze that seemed to see deep into her soul. "Besides, I know the truth."

Two

"The truth?" she repeated numbly, her heart throwing itself against her rib cage like some crazed inmate in county lockdown.

It wasn't impossible to believe he'd found out the truth about Theo. It just seemed so unlikely that he'd been here this long without mentioning it before now.

His slow, calculated smile didn't ease her concerns.

"Yes. The truth. I know why you're so afraid of telling this story."

"Oh. That truth." Her breath came out in a deep sigh. She turned away from him to conceal her relief, making a show of straightening the row of books at eye level.

"Lillian and Charles's story means too much to you. You're afraid you'll never do it justice."

"I suppose I am," she admitted. "After all, isn't that why the rest of you have been avoiding this project?"

She couldn't resist looking over her shoulder to see if her

barb hit home. For a moment he simply stared at her blankly. Then an amused smile curled his lips.

"This is why you need to write the script. No one else knows our family the way you do. No one else understands what this projects means to us—what it means to Lillian."

And just like that, his smile was gone, his gaze suddenly a dark, imploring blue.

"Oh, Jack Hudson, you do fight dirty, don't you?"

"I do when it means this much to someone I care about."

And of course, he cared about Lillian. She was perhaps the one woman in the world he did care about. Worse still, he knew Cece loved her, too. And obviously he was willing to manipulate Cece's softer emotions to get just what he wanted.

This was exactly why she didn't let people see those softer emotions very often.

"Come on, Cece. I know you don't want to see me beg."

"Maybe that's exactly what I want."

Again, he flashed her that charming smile of his. The one that had first won her young, impressionable heart all those years ago. Playfully, he dropped to his knees and shuffled forward a step or two, his fingers intertwined as he pleaded.

"Oh, get up," she snapped. He always had had a flair for the dramatic. The whole darn family had.

"If you care about Lillian at all, you'll take the job."

She wasn't ready to agree yet. Needing to buy herself more thinking time, she asked, "Just out of curiosity, why did she send you?"

He shrugged. "I'm Project Development Manager. This is what I do."

"Then she doesn't know?"

"About us?" Only the faintest hint of emotion crossed his face. Still he answered. "No. Is that why you've avoided

Lillian and everyone else for the past three years? Because you thought I'd told them about our affair?"

"I…"

She had assumed he'd told everyone. And the thought of the handsome, powerful Hudsons all knowing how she'd trailed after him like a lovesick puppy, how she'd begged him to admit he loved her, how she needed him… Well, it was enough to make any sane woman turn tail and scram.

But that was only the tip of the iceberg when it came to reasons she'd been avoiding the Hudsons.

Yes, Jack had broken her heart into a trillion tiny pieces. And yes, the thought of their ill-fated love affair still tortured her with burning humiliation—not to mention angst.

But the truth was, she blamed herself for that as much as she blamed him. More so, really.

She knew him, knew what she was getting into when they'd started sleeping together. Knew he was way out of her league. Knew that he dated movie stars and supermodels. That some of the most beautiful women in the world begged him for dates. She on the other hand, had features that might pass for marginally pretty anywhere else in the country, but in Hollywood, put her in the doesn't-even-warrant-a-second-glance category.

More to the point, she knew how troubled his youth had been. His parents' disastrous marriage had culminated with his mother's tragic death. He had more familial issues than she did. And *he* hadn't been going to therapy for them since he was three. She knew he didn't trust women and didn't believe in marriage. She knew all of that. And still she'd gone and fallen in love with him.

So who was really to blame here?

Besides, the truth was, none of that nonsense about her broken heart and wounded pride was the reason she'd been avoiding Jack.

No, the real reason was Theo, the son she'd borne Jack. The son he didn't know he had. A few months after their affair, when she'd found out she was pregnant, she decided never to tell Jack. She'd been living in France with no plans to ever return to the States. At the time, the decision had seemed logical. Looking back, it seemed childish. Spiteful, even.

But there was no undoing a decision like that. If Jack ever found out the truth, who knew what he might do?

No, it was like that moment in *Speed* when they decide to jump the bus over the gap in the highway. She had to bury her fear and doubts along with the love she'd once felt for Jack. Once the decision had been made, she'd had no choice but to hit the gas and hurtle forward toward her fate without looking back.

A day didn't go by that she didn't regret her decision. He had unwittingly given her the greatest gift she'd ever had. And she'd knowingly robbed him of the same.

Not only would he never forgive her, she'd never forgive herself. She couldn't possibly make it up to him by telling him the truth. Frankly, she was too terrified that he'd try to take Theo away from her in retaliation. But there was something she could do. She could write this script for him.

Professionally, it would be a huge stretch. But then she might at least begin to forgive herself for what she'd done.

Finally, she nodded. "I'll do it."

And if she played her cards right, Jack and Theo wouldn't even meet.

Jack grinned, standing. "I knew you would."

She didn't doubt it. Jack had plenty of failings, but lack of confidence wasn't one of them.

"Lillian has planned one of her big family dinners for tomorrow night. She's planning on your being there."

He issued the invitation—if it could be called that— casually as he headed for the door.

"Too bad I can't make it. I have other plans." A blatant lie, since her only plans on a Tuesday night were getting Theo to bed on time.

"Cancel them."

"I can't, Jack. Sorry."

He pinned her with a searing stare. "I'm sure whoever it is you're seeing can be put off. After all, this is business."

"It's not a date." Was that relief she saw in his expression? Surely not.

"Date or not, I'm sure you can cancel it," he insisted.

As loath as she was to bring it up, she didn't see any other choice. "It's my son."

"Oh, right, you have a son." He said it with the kind of casual disregard of someone completely unfamiliar with children and their needs.

"My nanny works only during the day—she has a family of her own," Cece found herself explaining. "And it'd be impossible to get a sitter this late. Sorry, it's impossible."

Jack frowned, shoving his hands deep into his pockets. "Well, bring him along."

If the idea hadn't been so repulsively terrifying, she might have laughed. Her rambunctious, talkative son at an elegant family dinner at Hudson Manor? And by family dinner, she assumed what Jack had meant was a working family dinner during which they would sequester themselves in the dining room to discuss a project for five or six hours.

"Um, no. I don't think so."

"Find a way to make it, Cece. It's important to Lillian. She wants to get started picking your brain about the script right away."

Cece waved a dismissive hand. "There's plenty of time for that after we go to contract. You know I'm not going to get started before then anyway."

"This time you will. We start shooting in two months."

"Two months? Are you crazy? I can't do a script like this in two months."

"Well, you'll have to. Lillian wants the film released on the sixtieth anniversary of the studio's opening. So we're working on a tight timetable."

Cece felt a scowl settling over her face as she did some quick mental calculations. Number of pages per day, times number of working days in the time frame, adding in days for revisions, backtracking and goof-ups.

She crossed her arms over her chest and glared at him. "I *might* be able to get it done."

"I knew you could."

"But you know you Hudsons should really plan better. You've all been living and breathing this industry since before you could crawl. You know these things take time."

"Come to dinner tomorrow night and you can suitably chastise all of us," he said as he finally left.

"I just might do that."

Of course, she would have to. If she really was going to get the script done in less that two months, she'd literally have to start working on Wednesday morning. Which meant she had just another day and a half to finish tweaking her current project.

The good news was, talking to Jack had helped her realize the current script's problem. She obviously hadn't spent enough time torturing her characters.

Just as she was shutting the front door, she heard the *slap-slap-slap* of bare toddler feet running on her Saltillo tiles, followed by the *clickety-clack* of the soles of Maria's shoes.

"Sorry, Cece. He slipped away from me."

Theo threw himself against her legs as if they'd been separated for weeks instead of mere minutes.

"No worries," she said, and she reached down to scoop Theo up into her arms.

"What that man?" Theo asked, looking at the door.

"Who was that man," she corrected automatically. "That was no one."

Theo frowned as he processed her answer, his tiny brow knitting in confusion. "I meet that man?"

"No. You've never met that man." Saying the words, she felt a pang deep in her heart. To offset it, she held Theo tight to her chest, propping her chin on top of his head and inhaling deeply. "And you never will."

She squeezed her eyes closed against the prickling of tears, as she was flooded with all the emotions she'd been ignoring for the past hour—all the fear, trepidation and guilt. Except for the one emotion she least wanted to examine. Her longing.

Jack scanned Lillian's sitting room in confusion. "Where is everyone?"

Instead of the loud and energetic crowd of Hudsons he expected, he found only Lillian.

Lillian looked around the empty room with mock surprise. "Why, Jack, what do you mean?"

"Grandmother, you wanted me to invite Cece to a family dinner tonight."

"Indeed. I did."

"But you didn't invite any other family members." He knew he was stating the obvious. It was never fun being manipulated by your grandmother. Worse still was the fear that Lillian was doing a little matchmaking. As if he hadn't been dreading tonight enough already.

"Of course I didn't. How would we get any serious work done if the whole family was here?"

"The way we always get work done when the whole

family is here," he stated blandly. "It's what we do. We're Hudsons. We work."

Lillian raised her chin regally. It was a gesture that gave him the impression she was looking down her nose at him despite the fact that she was five inches shorter than he was. "There's nothing wrong with having a strong work ethic, my boy."

"I didn't say—"

"You implied it. That, however, is not the point. It's been over three years since Cece has been to visit. If the whole family were here, she and I wouldn't get a moment to ourselves to discuss the project. That's why I didn't invite anyone else. Besides, I think between the three of us, we can find more than enough to talk about."

There were moments—and this was one of them—when Jack would have sworn his grandmother could see straight into his soul. That she saw past all the lies and nonsense to who he was at his deepest core. And that she knew the secrets he hid there.

It was disconcerting to say the least.

"Jack, dear," she said as she lowered herself to the edge of her cushioned ladder-back chair. "Please stop pacing. You're giving me motion sickness just watching you."

"I'm not pacing." But then he realized he must have been, because he had stopped to say it. "I was merely walking."

"When one walks around a room at a brisk clip, it's called pacing. And it's making my head spin. Besides which, you don't want to scare off poor Cece with all your prowling around, do you? I can't imagine why you're so nervous."

He nearly insisted that he wasn't nervous, but realized how repetitive it sounded. Instead, he crossed to the bar on the far side of the room and poured two glasses of sherry. Like all of Hudson Manor, Lillian's sitting room was decorated in the elegant French provincial style Lillian loved.

"If I were nervous, I doubt anyone would blame me," he observed as he made his way back across the room. "You've made it clear this project is the most important one we've ever worked on. It's a tremendous amount of pressure."

The double doors swung open, just in time for Cece to hear his words.

"I thought you Hudsons thrived on pressure."

For a moment, Cece stood there, framed by the double doors. She wore her thick brown hair up in a kind of twisted knot that managed to look both elegant and simple. A few silken strands hung loose, curling around her long, slender neck. Her sundress tied at the back of her neck and left her shoulders bare. Cinched with a wide black ribbon just under her breasts and with a full skirt that ended just below her knees, the dress highlighted her petite but curvaceous figure. The white fabric was covered with large red-and-black polka dots. Strappy heels added a good three inches to her height. In heels like that, she might even reach his chin.

At the sight of her standing there, so lovely and poised, every cell in his body tightened. She looked gorgeous in the dress, but he didn't like it. When they'd dated, she'd always dressed casually—jeans, tank tops. Better yet, nothing at all. When he'd seen her the day before, he could have sworn she hadn't aged a day since they broke up. But now she looked like an elegant stranger. It simultaneously reminded him that she'd moved on and that he wanted to strip her naked.

There was nothing more annoying than wanting the person you'd left years ago.

Thankfully, Lillian stood as Cece entered the room, holding out her hands to her goddaughter. "My dear, you look simply wonderful."

Cece smiled as she took Lillian's hands and kissed her cheek. "It's good to see you."

"It's nice to see you out of those tomboyish jeans you're always wearing."

Cece winked gamely. "I thought the occasion warranted getting dressed up." Her gaze scanned the room, briefly met his and then returned to Lillian's. She arched her eyebrow. "So then, it's not a family dinner. I thought a whole bunch of Hudsons still called the Manor home."

"Markus and Sabrina are dining with the Spielbergs," Lillian explained. "Dev's working late, and Bella is out with friends."

"Why do I get the feeling I'm the victim of a bait-and-switch scheme?" Cece asked.

Lillian shook her head with a sigh. "Apparently Jack didn't think I alone would be enough to lure you all the way out to Hudson Manor. He thought you wouldn't want to have dinner with an old woman like me."

"That's what Jack thought, is it?"

As Cece allowed Lillian to guide her over to the sofa, she sent a second surreptitious glance in Jack's direction. A scowl had settled over his handsome features, but he wiped it away before Lillian could see it. By the time he handed a sherry first to Lillian and then to her, a charming smile graced his lips, though it hadn't yet reached his eyes. For someone who had lobbied so hard to get her here, he did not look pleased to see her.

"I'm just surprised he invited you, Lillian," she said drolly. "He looks so eager to get me alone."

Lillian chuckled. "He does look a bit as if he's been sentenced to death, doesn't he?"

Even with his features etched with dread, he looked damned good. Handsome devil.

She took a sip of the sherry Jack had handed her and a wave of nostalgia washed over her. There was an old-world formality to everything Lillian did. Drinks before dinner—sherry no less—typified that. Even as a teenager, whenever she and her family dined here, she was allowed a small glass of sherry. Sipping it now brought her straight back to all those many dinners of her youth.

Visiting Hudson Manor was one of the few times her parents always got along. No matter what else was happening, they called a truce around Lillian and Charles. As a result, she had fond memories of Hudson Manor, even if they were bittersweet.

It made her glad she'd dressed up for tonight's dinner, even though she'd had to raid her neighbor's closet to do it.

When Jack returned with his own drink—a tumbler of Patrón, no doubt—he gave her dress an appreciative once-over. So he wouldn't think she'd dressed up for him, she said to Lillian, "I remembered from my childhood that you always dressed for dinner."

"Not every dinner," Lillian said, "Only the important ones. And—"

"Any time family and friends are together, it's important."

Cece and Jack spoke at the same time, finishing the sentence for Lillian. It was a sentiment she'd drilled into the heads of her children and grandchildren. As evidenced by the fact that both Cece and Jack remembered it now. Their eyes met and laughter passed between them. For a moment, it felt almost as though they were friends again. Allies, navigating these complicated waters together.

Suddenly it wasn't just the sherry she felt nostalgic for. She longed for the simplicity of their childhood years together, scampering over the grounds of Hudson Manor, climbing oak trees and hiding from their parents. For the intimacy of the months they'd spent together three years ago. For the way they'd lounge together on her sofa reading industry gossip online. For the warmth of his body spooned against hers late at night.

The moment passed the instant Lillian spoke.

"Jack told me you were planning on bringing your son. Theodore, isn't it? So why didn't you?"

Cece dragged her gaze from Jack's. "I was able to find a babysitter after all." And now she owed her neighbor, Marissa, not just for the dress but for an evening having her ear talked off as well.

"A babysitter?" Lillian frowned. "In my opinion, young people now don't spend enough time with their children. You should have brought him."

"Trust me, Lillian, I spend plenty of time with Theo. He's rarely more than fifteen feet from my side. Besides, you were one of the original working mothers. You made movies throughout Markus's and David's childhoods."

"Well, you can't blame me for trying." Lillian smiled, aware she'd been caught. "After all, since none of my grandchildren seem inclined to procreate, your Theo may be the closest thing I have to a great-grandchild of my own."

Regret stabbed at her. She'd known what she was depriving Jack of. But somehow she'd justified it to herself. After all, Jack had no interest in being a father—he'd certainly made that clear enough when they'd been dating. But until this moment, it never occurred to her that she was also depriving Lillian of a great-grandchild.

Leaning forward, she placed her hand on Lillian's. The other woman's skin felt paper thin and soft in its brittle fragility. Her metacarpal bones stood in sharp relief against the flesh of her hand.

Sadness followed quickly on the heels of her regret.

Lillian's growing old, Cece realized as she took in the near-transparent quality of Lillian's skin. Her face, which had always seemed ageless, was now lined with deep grooves. Her hair—always thick and lush—now seemed wispy. *How did I not notice before now? How did I not see this coming?*

She supposed it was because Lillian had always seemed so larger than life. Suddenly the time Cece had spent in voluntary exile seemed far too long.

"I'll bring Theo by for a visit sometime soon."

Lillian's lined face broke into a wide smile. "Then Jack didn't tell you?"

"Tell me what?" Cece shot Jack an appraising look, but his countenance was as distant and reserved as always.

"That while you're working on the script, we want you and Theo to move into Hudson Manor."

Three

"You want me to move into Hudson Manor?"

"Yes."

"But…but…" Cece sputtered uselessly, resisting the urge to repeat the question yet again. Nothing like a professional word-smith who couldn't form a coherent thought. "That's crazy!"

Yes. That was much better.

Jack's lips twitched as if he were secretly amused.

Obviously he wasn't going to be helpful. Cece turned to Lillian. "You can't be serious."

But instead of answering, Lillian stood on slightly unsteady feet. "You know, dear, I'm not sure I'm up to dinner after all. I think I'll just have Hannah bring a tray to my room."

Cece jumped up, putting a hand on Lillian's arm. "You can't leave."

But Lillian ignored her protestations. "It was wonderful to see you."

"Yes, of course, but about moving in—"

"Jack can arrange everything. You'll have plenty of time over dinner to sort it all out. And Hannah can prepare rooms for you first thing in the morning. The third floor is empty these days. I'm sure there's plenty of room for you and Theo there."

All of her additional protests were brushed aside as well, with Lillian making her way out the door and Cece all but clinging to her legs, begging her to stay. Anything to avoid being alone with Jack.

Yet despite her efforts, a moment later, Lillian was gone and they were alone. Annoyed and wanting someone to blame it on, Cece turned to Jack, hands propped on her hips, her gaze shrewd and assessing.

"Did you know she was going to do this?"

He drank the last of his tequila and set the empty tumbler on the side bar. "Did I know she was going to ask you to move in or that she'd leave us alone for dinner?"

"Either."

"No to the first. Yes to the second."

She could only hope Lillian wasn't doing a little matchmaking. What a disappointment that would be for everyone involved. Rather than bring up that possibility, Cece said to Jack, "She can't seriously expect me to move in while I write the script."

"You have to admit, living here would have advantages."

"You're on board with this idea?" She forced herself to sit on the settee.

"Why wouldn't I be?"

"Because the idea is crazy." She threw up her hands in disgust, ruining the illusion of calm sophistication she'd been trying to maintain.

"So you keep saying."

"I can't move into Hudson Manor."

"You wouldn't be moving in, it's only temporary."

"I don't care how temporary it is." Her voice rose as panic crept in, edging out her logic. She could feel herself getting sucked back into his life. "I can't live here."

"Why not?"

"For starters, I have a son—"

"—who can stay here just as easily as he can anywhere else."

She couldn't stop shaking her head in mute denial. Part of her expected Jack to start chuckling, to admit how half-baked the idea was. But he didn't. He just kept watching her with that silent appraising stare, waiting for her to give in.

She stifled the feeling of dread that she might. The silence stretched between them; the ticking of Lillian's clock on the fireplace mantel seemed overly loud.

"I can't just uproot Theo and cart him all the way down here to live for a few months."

"He's a child, not a redwood," Jack noted wryly. "I doubt he'll be too traumatized."

"Really, Jack? Child-rearing advice? From you?"

He shrugged to acknowledge the irony. "Even I know the difference between a kid and a tree. Besides, it's not like he's never been away from home before, right? Think of it like a vacation."

She searched his face, looking for any sign of the Jack she'd once known so well. Every once in a while, she saw a flash of heat in his gaze, as if he, too, was still haunted by the memory of their time together. As if he, too, still felt the stirring of desire. But before she could decipher his mood, the moment would pass and he'd once more be the cool stranger who'd shown up on her doorstep the day before.

She let out a nervous chuckle. "Except it's not a vacation. And this isn't exactly a Holiday Inn, now is it?"

"Sure, it's a bit big, but—"

"The thing is, Jack, I work hard to protect Theo. I don't want him to have the kind of childhood I had."

The lines around his mouth tightened. "Your childhood wasn't that bad."

Obviously he was thinking of his own childhood. She had to smother the protective maternal instincts his expression roused. She wanted to brush her hand over his forehead, smooth away the tension of his frown. But of course, touching Jack, even to comfort him, had gotten her in trouble more than once. And the underlying tension between them was strong enough as it was.

"Compared to yours? No. It wasn't. At least I had both of my parents. And at least—most of the time—they were even together. Still, I don't want my son growing up in Hollywood, being dragged from location to location. Thrust into the care of whatever craft services person or best boy that happens to have a free hand. Falling asleep at two in the morning on the floor of the editing room."

"I don't think moving into Hudson Manor for two months so you can be closer to Lillian while you write entails any of those things."

"That's not what I meant. I just want him to have a normal childhood."

"Nobody has a *normal* childhood."

"Yeah, Jack, they do. Plenty of people do. They join Cub Scouts and play on the swings at the park. They go to story time at the library and have picnics in the backyard. Normal stuff. They don't live in grand mansions with servants. Even for a few short months."

"It's not going to kill him."

"I just don't see that it's necessary."

"That's because you're being stubborn."

As they spoke, he'd been circling his way around the room,

closing in on her. Short of jumping up and dashing for the door, there wasn't anywhere she could go. Certainly not without making it obvious just how nervous he was making her. Still, she was starting to feel like the sacrificial goat chained to the post in the T. Rex pen at the beginning of *Jurassic Park*.

She could tell she was losing the argument. Any minute now all that would be left of her objections was the dangling chain that had once been attached to her neck.

"I'm not being stubborn, I'm just trying to protect my son."

Suddenly he was there, just a step away, really. Close enough that when he reached out to tip up her chin, he didn't even have to stretch out his arm to do so.

"You know what I think?"

His eyes searched her face and as much as she wanted to look away, she found herself being sucked into that crystal-blue gaze of his. Found herself getting lost in anticipation. She wanted him to kiss her. She wanted to believe that beneath his cool facade he was as drawn to her as she was to him.

But instead of kissing her, he said, "I think you're doing this to spite me."

"To spite you?"

"Yes." He brushed her chin with his thumb, tantalizingly close to her mouth but not touching it. "You know this is important to me. So you're being difficult on purpose."

She swatted away his hand. "Don't be ridiculous."

"Then what's really going on here?"

"I just don't think it's necessary. The real reason you want me here is so that you can keep an eye on me. You're going to be breathing down my neck nonstop. My creative process—"

But before she could go off on a rant, Jack interrupted her. "The truth is, Lillian doesn't like to admit it, but she's not as strong as she used to be."

"Oh." Cece rocked backward feeling as if she'd had the wind knocked out of her. "I didn't realize."

"I can only assume it's why she wants you nearby. She doesn't get out very often."

"But—"

"It's not like you can just meet her at the Starbucks on the corner every time you want to pick her brain."

"I can drive out here when I need to talk to her," Cece protested weakly. She was losing this argument and she knew it. If Lillian was as frail as Jack made her sound, then Cece would have to give in.

"You live in Santa Barbara. If traffic's bad, that's two, two and a half hours each way. You'd spend half the day in the car. You won't be getting as much work done as you need to and you'll be away from your son. No, this is the only way."

"Damn it. I hate that you're right." If she drove back and forth to interview Lillian, either she'd never get the work done in time or she'd never see her son.

Neither alternative was acceptable. Despite what Jack seemed to believe, she wanted the project to be a success. She also wanted to keep him as far away from Theo as possible.

And—if she was honest with herself—as far away from her as possible, too. Her heart was still far too vulnerable to the likes of Jack Hudson.

A fact that was illustrated all too clearly by the way her heart rate picked up when Jack flashed her a cocky grin.

"I knew I'd convince you."

"Of course you did," she said drily.

"I'll make sure you don't regret it."

"I already do."

But, on the bright side, it wasn't as if Jack still lived at Hudson Manor. He had his own place in Malibu. Given their history, he probably wasn't any more eager to spend time with her than she was with him. So he was unlikely to stop by just to hang out. She was no more likely to run into Jack at Hudson Manor than she was at her own home.

Chances were good that she and Theo could move into the third floor and live there for the next few months without Jack and Theo ever meeting. She'd just have to make sure that if Jack ever did come to visit, Theo was tucked safely away in their rooms. This could work. She'd make it work. She had to.

Feeling perhaps overly optimistic, she stood, setting aside her sherry glass.

"You're not leaving already?"

He sounded almost disappointed.

"I need to go home and start packing," she pointed out. "Lillian expects me in the morning."

"But you haven't even eaten."

Funny, she felt as if her convictions had already been served up on a silver tray.

"I'm not staying for dinner."

"Well, you should. Hannah makes some of the best braised lamb you've ever had."

She had to suppress a snort of irony. Just now she felt a little too much sympathy for those slaughtered lambs. "I think I'll pass."

Jack seemed ready to protest, but she booked it out of there before he could make any headway. Damn those pesky Hudsons who refused to take no for an answer.

She was still cursing hours later, as she sat on the side of her son's bed stroking his hair.

The inky locks curled over his forehead and against his cheeks. It was time for another haircut, she mused as she ran her fingers through the shaggy length.

He had his father's hair, dark and springy, with a hint of

curl to it. Her own hair was similar in texture, but more brown than black.

Theo's eyes fluttered open. "Mommy?"

"Yes, honey? I'm here." Unable to resist, she lowered the bed rail and laid down beside him in his twin bed.

He'd always been tall for his age and she'd gotten rid of the crib as soon as he'd started trying to climb out of it. Now he rolled closer to her, cuddling next to her and rubbing his cheek against her shoulder. "Read me book," he mumbled.

"Sure, honey." But he was already back asleep.

Laying there in the dark, with the only light coming from the single bulb out in the hall, Cece felt the weight of the past few days bearing down on her.

What had she gotten herself into?

Three years ago, when she'd decided to raise her baby all on her own, without ever telling Jack he was a father, she'd known that her decision meant she could never again associate with the Hudsons.

It had seemed a small enough price to pay. Yes, in many ways, they were like family. And, yes, she'd practically grown up with them. But they were also overbearing, domineering, presumptuous.

And since Jack, to whom she'd always been closest, had just broken her heart, the thought of never seeing them again held more than a little appeal.

She'd never imagined that she'd miss them. That someday she might regret her decision.

Of course, she'd also never imagined how motherhood would feel. How it would transform her so completely. That she might regret depriving Jack of that experience.

But at least she could rest easy in the knowledge that fatherhood was the very last thing Jack wanted. He'd made that clear enough when they'd been together. He had absolutely no interest in marriage or family.

She remembered the moment as clearly as if it had been yesterday. They were lying together in bed, late on a Sunday morning. They were at her house, piled into the tiny full-size bed that just fit into her subcompact master bedroom. They always stayed at her house even though his house in Malibu was much larger.

Still, it was cozy, snuggled under the covers, mugs of coffee on the nightstand beside a bowl of cherries and buttered slices of baguette. He'd been wearing a dusky blue T-shirt and jogging shorts, because he'd been the one to go out for coffee. Cherry juice stained his lips red—Jack had always had ridiculously lush lips for a man.

He'd woken her up with kisses, sliding his hand under the white tank she wore to bed, feeding her cherries to lure her from sleep. Still she'd protested, yanking the covers up over his head.

And it was there, cocooned in that midmorning light, surrounded by the musky scent of his warmth, with the sweet taste of cherries still on her lips, that she said it.

"If I could wake up like this every day, maybe I wouldn't mind mornings so much."

"Every day?" he'd asked.

He'd stilled instantly, but her internal alarm telling her that she'd screwed up didn't start ringing until after she said, "Yep. Every day for the rest of my life."

That's when she noticed that his hand was no longer caressing her breast, that his shoulders had tensed.

She opened her eyes to study his face. Sunlight filtered through the sheets casting his features in a soft glow completely at odds with the rigid distaste of his expression.

That moment right there was the beginning of the end.

Within ten minutes, he'd left her house. Within ten days, they had "the big talk," during which he told her that—while the sex was phenomenally great—he never intended for their relationship to be anything but sex.

Stupidly, she hadn't believed he really meant it. Until a week later when one of the scandal sheets snapped pictures of him cozying up with the starlet from Hudson Pictures' latest blockbuster. He hadn't even bothered to deny the allegations.

What followed was the kind of big, nasty breakup she'd sworn she'd never be a part of. In short, the kind of thing her parents had done every couple of years.

She'd yelled. He'd denied nothing. She'd thrown things. He hadn't even ducked. She'd cried. He'd quietly packed up the toothbrush, razor and half a drawer's worth of clothes that had accumulated at her house.

To this day, she was embarrassed by how emotional she'd been in the face of his cool disinterest. Her only excuse was that she'd been eight weeks pregnant. She hadn't known it at the time, but surely that was excuse enough if she needed one.

Her behavior since then was perhaps less excusable.

Now, lying beside her son, propped up on her elbow as she watched him sleep, she wondered how she'd ever thought she could pull this off. And yet, so far she had. When she'd returned from France a year and a half ago with her "adopted" son, no one had seen through her lie. The question was, could she bring Theo to Hudson Manor without raising suspicion?

Tomorrow she'd find out.

Being back in Cece's little Santa Barbara bungalow roused more memories than Jack wanted to deal with early on a Wednesday morning. Let alone before coffee.

That, he told himself, was his sole motive in stopping at Starbucks on the way to Cece's. It was only logical to pick up a Venti mocha for her when he bought his own double espresso. This, he assured himself, was only feeding his own need for caffeine. It was not a peace offering.

Still, he felt oddly disconcerted while he waited for her to open the door. Strangely barraged by memories he wasn't quite prepared to deal with. When he'd been here two days ago, he'd managed to push aside the memories. To keep them deeply buried, as he usually did.

But this morning, standing on her doorstep with the two cups of coffee in hand, he couldn't help remembering all the times he'd woken early, gone out for a run and swung by Starbucks on the way back. On those mornings, he hadn't waited on the doorstep for her to answer the door. He'd let himself in with his key. Cece—a consummate night owl, often working well past midnight—would invariably still be in bed.

Bringing her coffee and the occasional croissant, crawling back into bed himself after his shower and waiting for her to rouse…those were some of the best memories of their time together. Hell, those were some of the best memories of his life.

If he were honest with himself, he still wanted her. Still yearned for her. Still woke up late at night haunted by the memory of what it had been like to hold her in his arms. To sink into her body and find release.

Breaking up with her had been the hardest thing he'd ever done. He'd managed it only by carefully burying every shred of emotion. By never, ever being honest with himself.

Not exactly the kind of issue he wanted to examine while waiting on her doorstep. Or ever, really.

Though he'd made a point of not arriving at her house too early today, he still fully expected her to only now be getting up. Once he rang the bell, he was prepared to wait for a good ten minutes or so before she made it to the door.

So he was surprised when he heard a sort of scuffling

rumble from the other side of the door. Then he heard a high-pitched voice shout, "I get! I get!"

Jack frowned, listening to the unmistakable sound of someone fumbling with the doorknob. He waited, expecting the door to open. But one moment stretched into another. The fumbling sounds continued followed by the click of the latch on the door releasing. As the front door swung open, he heard a thunder of footsteps.

And then Cece's voice. "Theo, no!"

The door continued to swing open carried by its momentum. In the foyer beyond, he saw Cece crouched beside a small boy, lecturing him fiercely.

"You can't open the front door, Theo, even if there's someone knocking on it. Even if you think it's Maria. Even if—"

She broke off the instant she looked up to see him standing there. She was dressed in her standard jeans and T-shirt—this pair even rattier than the outfit she'd had on the day before yesterday. Her hair was pulled back into a scraggly ponytail from which several strands had already escaped. A smudge of something mysterious streaked her cheek. In short, she looked delightfully rumpled.

And somehow, even though he'd seen her just yesterday, he was completely unprepared for his body's visceral response to her. For the way his pulse thundered and his body tightened.

He'd never understood how she made a T-shirt and jeans so damn sexy. In a town of slender, long-limbed women, Cece was shorter and far curvier than the current definition of beauty. Yet for the past three years, her body had been the gold standard against which every other woman he'd dated had been measured. No one else had measured up. No one else had even come close.

And, God help him, he still wanted her. No, *wanted* was too tame a word. He craved her. Like something he was addicted to. Like coffee. Or air.

She jerked to standing, pulling the boy close to her side, her expression registering shock. "What are you doing here?"

He held out the Venti mocha. "I brought coffee."

Rather than taking it from him, she knelt by her son and said, "Theo, go into the other room."

However, the boy wouldn't be deterred. He wiggled free from Cece's grasp and dashed toward the door.

At least, Jack thought he was dashing for the door. Instead the boy launched himself at Jack's legs, squeezing them into a tight brusque hug.

"Hel-woo!" the boy pronounced when he stepped back. The boy's hair was dark and wavy, his eyes a brilliant and piercing blue, his smile a mouthful of crooked baby teeth. He bounced up and down as he spoke. "We go vacation!"

Jack looked up at Cece, handing over the coffee. "So, this is your son."

Four

Our son.

Of course, that wasn't what he said. Jack said *your son*. But somehow, the words that echoed in her mind were *our son*.

Her breath caught in her chest. Literally. She couldn't breathe out. The air was trapped in her lungs, making her feel simultaneously as if her lungs were going to explode and she was going to suffocate.

She just stood, still as stone—the only movement of her body her pounding heart—waiting for him to look into Theo's eyes and know the truth.

The moment stretched endlessly. She was sure he'd see it. He couldn't possibly miss it. She waited for a burst of anger. An accusation. A reprisal. Anything.

And then she noticed the cup of coffee he still held extended, calmly waiting for her to take it from him.

She straightened slowly, reaching for the coffee with the

same steady, cautious movement she used when sneaking a glass over the spiders that occasionally wandered inside. She had a strict catch-and-release policy when it came to spiders. While she appreciated their contribution to the ecosystem, she did not want them in her home.

Not unlike her feelings for Jack, she realized as she accepted the coffee.

Her first instinct—to order Theo from the room—nearly caused hysterical laughter to bubble up. At twenty-three months, Theo rarely followed directions and met orders of any kind with a headstrong obstinacy that she blamed on Jack. Lord knew she'd never been so stubborn and willful as a child. Since she didn't have the time to gently coax Theo into the other room without arising suspicion, she followed her second instinct, to get Jack out of her house quickly and without incident. Now, if only she could find a really big glass and a piece of cardboard to slide under his feet and trap him inside of it.

"Thanks for the coffee, but why are you here?"

"I came to help you pack up your stuff."

"Ah." As if this were a perfectly ordinary task for a movie studio exec. "And why would you do that?"

While they spoke, she'd been trying to subtly angle Theo behind her. It had been futilely optimistic of her to try. Theo dashed around her legs to run in circles around them. "Pack. Pack. Pack. Pack," he chanted.

Jack watched with the sort of stunned bemusement most single guys bestowed upon Theo. "He's certainly…"

"Full of energy?" she supplied. "Rambunctious? Energetic?"

"I was going to say smart."

A little burst of pride filled her. "He certainly is. Most people don't see it, though."

"I imagine they're distracted by the blur of motion and constant noise."

Theo continued to chant, though the refrain of "Pack. Pack. Pack," had been transformed into "Back pack. Pack back."

She couldn't help but be a little amused by Theo's song as well as Jack's obvious confusion. "You were probably—" she began before abruptly breaking off.

You were probably like that as a child, was what she'd been about to say. Thank God she'd caught herself in time.

"Yes?" Jack prodded.

She looked up to find him studying her. Her heart pounding, she finished, "Were probably just in the neighborhood."

It was an asinine thing to say, but hopefully he wouldn't give her stupidity too much thought.

He just gave her a look that indicated he thought her brain must have been scrambled by too much time with an energetic two-year-old. As if to reinforce the idea, Theo dashed from the room.

"I just thought I could help out," Jack said.

"Well, you're too late," she said to Jack. "We're mostly packed. I planned on leaving for Hudson Manor just as soon as traffic dies down."

Of course, this was L.A. Traffic never died down. What she'd really meant was as soon as she worked up the courage.

As if he could see right through her lie, Jack quirked an eyebrow. He seemed to be inviting her to join in on the joke. He looked so sexy standing there, she felt her heart rate kick up a notch. She'd missed him so much. And not just the sex, either.

She'd missed their camaraderie. Their companionship. And as crazy as it sounded, she missed things they hadn't even had. Their relationship, with its unique combination of friendship and sex, had held the promise of growing into something truly wonderful. It had the potential to become something deeper and more emotional.

She'd wanted that kind of relationship for them. If she was honest with herself, she still wanted it.

Oh, he was too tempting.

Just then, a series of thumps and scrapes heralded Theo's return. He came through the living room, dragging his tricycle with all of his thirty-pound strength.

"Bring bike?" he asked.

As much as she wanted to keep them separated, she found herself welcoming the distraction.

"No."

Theo's forehead furrowed. "No?"

She could practically see the little wheels turning in his mind as he calculated the best approach. He went straight for the tears.

His tiny lower lip quivered as his eyes pooled with tears. "No bike?"

There was even a little waver in his voice. His grandparents would be proud of his performance. Which was stronger, she wondered wryly, his grandmother's acting skills or his grandfather's sense of dramatic timing?

"No," she said firmly, with the resolution that came from having witnessed countless such tragic displays. "No bike. There isn't room in the car for it."

"I've got room in my car."

Cece glared at Jack. Unfortunately, he didn't notice, being too entranced by the magic of Theo's whole-face grin.

"Bike!" Theo leaped with glee.

"No bike," she repeated firmly, hoping to get an upper hand before she lost control completely. "You won't have anywhere to ride it."

Though her explanation was as much for Jack as it was for Theo, Jack didn't seem to notice. Nor did he notice her pointed look or her exaggerated back-me-up-on-this tone.

"Have you forgotten about all those patios? There's plenty of room."

"I'm going there to work," she reminded Jack. "I won't have time to take him out to ride his bike."

"I'll do it."

Theo looked back and forth from her to Jack, obviously trying to gauge whether or not Jack held enough sway over his mother to be a useful ally. He must have decided it was worth the investment, because he once again smiled brightly at Jack and chirped, "Bike!"

"Great." Her sarcasm was lost on Theo, but not on Jack. Theo dashed from the hallway—no doubt to find more toys he could talk Jack into carting across town for him. She just glared at Jack. "Remind me again why you're here."

"I'm here to help you pack up." Jack sent her a questioning look. "You don't want me here, though, do you?"

Of course she didn't *want* him here. She'd been banking on the fact that he wouldn't be anywhere near Hudson Manor. "I'm just surprised you're here. You could have sent some flunky to help pack up my stuff. This seems way beneath you."

"Right now, making sure you get the script for *Honor* done on time is my top priority."

"Which means?"

"Which means whatever you need, all you have to do is ask."

"Great." She tried to sound genuinely pleased, really she did. 'Cause let's face it, there was nothing more exciting than finding out the man you used to be in love with is spending time with you only because he's a micromanager.

But he must have heard the resignation in her voice. "You don't want me spending time with your son."

Jack stood with his hand tucked into his jeans' pocket. He wore a dark green T-shirt that accentuated the breadth of his shoulders and hinted at the muscles of his chest. Must be one of the downfalls of being insanely rich and ridiculously handsome. You looked too good, even when dressing down.

Of course, how good he looked was the least of her worries. There was probably no point in lying. "You're right. I don't want you spending time with Theo."

"Do you mind telling me why?"

As a matter of fact, she did mind. What was worse, the fear that he'd discover the truth about Theo or the faint glimmer of hope that stirred in her heart each time she saw Jack on her doorstep?

So she evaded the question. "Why don't we start by your telling me why I should be all fired up and excited by the prospect of your spending time with him?"

Jack frowned. "Do you really think I'm such a bad guy to be around?"

"Let's just say I don't think you're the most reliable guy."

He winced, but it was a faux, exaggerated wince, full of charm and fake contrition. "I suppose you think I deserved that."

"I think we'll get along better over the next couple of months if we don't talk about what I think you deserve."

"Fair enough." Then his expression grew serious. "You know I'd never hurt your son."

She must have imagined the faint glimmer of pain in his gaze. Yet despite all they'd been through, she couldn't stand the thought that she might actually be hurting his feelings. So she added, "I don't believe you'd intentionally hurt him, but he's a very sensitive boy. A few months from now you'll be out of our lives. And you'll hurt him just by not being there."

Jack studied her expression, his gaze thick with regret. "Cece, about—"

"Whatever it is you're about to say, you don't have to. Jack, I don't regret what happened between us."

"You don't?"

Of course she did. But the truth was far too complicated. So she stuck with the easy lie. "Of course not. I certainly hope you don't think I've been nursing a broken heart these last few years."

He looked chagrined. Clearly he'd believed exactly that.

Which was so annoying. Of course he'd broken her heart. But she'd *so* hoped he hadn't noticed. To hide the truth, she quickly rattled off all the benefits from their failed relationship.

"Think about it, Jack. If we hadn't broken up, I never would have moved to France. I never would have spent that time living with my mother. She wouldn't have gotten back into acting. I wouldn't have written *The Wave*. I wouldn't have adopted my son. In a lot of ways, breaking up with you is the best thing that ever happened to me."

"In that case," he said drily, "you should be encouraging me to spend time with him. After I desert him, he'll probably win the lottery."

She smiled, charmed despite herself. "Well, he doesn't buy many tickets."

"He should start. At any rate, I think we can both agree that my hanging around while he's riding his bike in the driveway isn't going to scar him for life."

Ah…see how neatly he'd trapped her? Jack was like that. Somehow he always managed to get his way. Always managed to trick her into doing what he wanted.

She narrowed her eyes and scowled at him. "Surely there must be something on the lot you could be doing."

"Nope, I'm all yours."

Cece bit down on her lip, swallowing a groan of frustration. How like Jack to sweep in and disrupt all her plans and silence all her objections. On the bright side, she knew how easily distracted Jack was. He couldn't possibly really be interested in spending time with Theo. As soon as she was living at Hudson Manor and deep into her work on the script, he'd forget he promised to hang out with Theo.

She could only hope that once Jack was back out of their lives, Theo would forget him as easily.

As Jack watched Theo running up the drive of Hudson Manor, Cece following him with her purse slung over one shoulder and her computer bag over the other, one question echoed through his mind. When the hell had he become a masochist?

Okay, Lillian wanted to make *Honor*. Fine. She wanted him to talk Cece into writing the script. Sure, he'd done it. She wanted him to lure Cece back to Hudson Manor. Yep, he'd even arranged that little miracle.

So shouldn't his job here be done? Shouldn't he be back in his office at the lot, answering e-mails, taking calls and peacefully waiting for Cece to deliver the script a couple of months from now?

That had been his plan. So where had he gone wrong? How exactly had he ended up driving across town with a muddy-wheeled bicycle, a beat-up red wagon and a bucket of bubbles on the passenger seat of his hundred-thousand-dollar Tesla Roadster?

Before he could come up with an answer, Cece turned around and looked over her shoulder to where he stood, hip propped on his driver-side door, watching her.

"Hey, slow poke," she called out. "Make yourself useful and grab a bag on your way up."

Her bright red Prius was parked in front of his own car. The trunk was popped to reveal two suitcases, a duffel bag and two plastic milk crates, one loaded with children's books, the other with reference books. He stacked one crate on top of the other.

"Be careful," she called out as he reached for them. "Those are both heavy."

He picked up the crates, stifled a groan and tried not to stagger under their weight. "Is this really necessary?"

"Don't look at me, this was your idea."

"I meant, was it really necessary to bring this many books?"

She shrugged as he caught up with her by the front door. "You want a writer to move, she brings books. It's the way of the world. You didn't have to try to be such a show-off and carry both at once."

"Trust me. I'm wishing now I hadn't."

He entered the door she held open for him, amazed at the way they'd fallen into such easy banter. It had always been like this between them. Relaxed. Fun. Both comforting and comfortable in a way nothing else in his life had ever been.

So why did her blasé manner annoy him so? Frankly, he should be relieved that she was making this easy for him. That she had such a healthy attitude about their breakup. That it was the best damn thing that had ever happened to her.

It shouldn't matter to him, but it did.

Three years ago, when he'd walked out of her life, he'd done it for her own good.

He'd grown up under the shadow of his parents' dismal marriage. For the first nine years of his life, he'd stood by while his father berated, manipulated and occasionally verbally abused his mother. After his mother's death, his father had proceeded to abandon his children, too, sending Jack's younger sister, Charlotte, to live with her maternal grandparents and leaving Jack in the care of Lillian and Charles.

Jack knew firsthand how destructive relationships could be. He'd sworn he'd never do that to someone he cared about. So as soon as Cece had hinted that what she felt for him was more than just sexual desire, he'd ended it.

At the time, he'd thought he was being self-sacrificing. It was the only time in his life he'd set aside his own needs for the sake of someone else. He'd felt damn near saintly.

He'd walked away to protect her heart. And now it seemed as if her heart wasn't in danger after all.

He strode up the walkway to the house, quickly closing the distance between them. By the time he reached her, she'd let herself in the front door. Theo ran through the foyer ahead of her, clutching a stuffed hippo nearly as large as he was.

"No, Theo, not that way," she called out. "Up the stairs."

Theo ignored her, only to plow straight into the waiting arms of Hannah, the Hudsons' longtime housekeeper. She swooped him up and held him out as if to inspect him. "Whoa there. This must be young Theo."

"Sorry, Hannah." Cece leaned around her son to plant a kiss on Hannah's cheek. "I'll try to keep him from tearing through the house."

"Nonsense. It's been far too long since we've had little ones around. They keep you young and we could all use a little of that."

Theo bicycled his legs in pantomime of running, like Wile E. Coyote suspended in midair. "Want down."

"Theo…" Cece chided.

"Peeease!" Theo smiled broadly.

Hannah all but melted. "Here ya go, boy." She set him down but held tight to his hand. "Let me show you up to your rooms on the third floor. Maybe running up and down all these stairs will tire you out so your mother can get her work done."

"More likely," Cece murmured, "chasing after him will tire me out."

"Looks like he's got Hannah wrapped around his finger already," Jack said as he set down the crates of books. He wasn't going to carry them upstairs until he knew where she wanted to set up her office.

Cece looked over her shoulder, her smile a mixture of amusement and nostalgia. "Hannah always was a sucker for you boys." She blanched, as if catching herself in a faux pas. "For boys, I mean. I mean, Hannah was always a sucker for boys."

Her sudden burst of nervous babbling intrigued him.

He stepped closer to her, not stopping until she had to tilt her head to look up at him. "If I didn't know better, I'd say you were nervous about being alone with me."

The teasing seemed to ease her nerves. She quirked an eyebrow. "Thank God you know better."

She moved to step away, but he stopped her, wrapping a hand around her arm. He waited until she looked up at him to ask the question that had been on his mind the whole drive over. "I have to admit, I'm surprised by how completely unaffected you claim you were by our breakup."

"Claim?" Annoyance flashed in her eyes. "That implies you don't believe me."

"Admit it. You were starting to fall for me."

He was an idiot for saying it. If she'd been lucky enough to escape from their affair unscathed, then he should be clapping her on the back and buying her drinks. Hell, he should be asking her how she'd done it, because he certainly hadn't been so lucky.

But instead of congratulating her, he stood there like a fool, waiting for some sign that their breakup had—at the very least—inconvenienced her.

"Why should I admit that? It's not true." Her expression softened to exaggerated sympathy. "Unless you need me to stroke your ego. Having a hard time with the ladies lately, are you?" She patted his hand to coddle him. "You're absolutely right. I was heartbroken."

He chuckled at her performance. And here she claimed her mother was the only one in the family with acting ability.

"Nice try, but I know the truth. You were hurt."

"I was offended." She rolled her eyes as she said it. Turning in mock disgust, she headed up the stairs herself.

He followed her, stopping her at the first landing. Her skin was warm under his hand. Her arm thin, but well muscled. Small but strong. That was Cece all over.

"I did it to protect you."

"From what?"

"I'm not good husband material. Hell, I'm not even good boyfriend material."

"Yeah, I know." She jerked her arm from his grasp. "And some men just make excuses because it's easier than sticking around long enough to see what they're made of."

There was a hint of bite to her words. Just enough for him to know that he really had hurt her three years ago. She made to turn away from him again, and again he stopped her.

"Either way, I'm sorry for the way things turned out."

She eyed him, suspicion seeming to war with her pride. Finally she gave a stiff little nod. Whatever stronger emotion he thought he saw in her gaze vanished and was replaced with an impish smile.

"Don't be," she teased. "Like I said earlier, it all worked out for the best. Besides…" Her expression grew thoughtful. "It's so much better this way, isn't it? No one got hurt—not really, anyway—and we're still friends, right?"

"Is that what we are?"

Her gaze searched his face. With unexpected tenderness, she reached up and traced a finger over his brow.

"No matter what happened, I always considered you my friend, Jack."

He caught her hand in his. "Is that why you've avoided me for the past three years?"

"I've hardly avoided you."

"Then what would you call it?"

"Bad luck, I guess. L.A.'s a big town, Jack. You live on one side, I live on the other. It shouldn't surprise anyone that our paths never cross. It's not like you were beating down my door, either."

"And what about your threat to never work for Hudson Pictures?"

"Obviously I've gotten over it or I wouldn't be here now. Whatever hard feelings I had for you, they're all in the past."

This time, when she turned to walk away, he let her go. He didn't know if she was lying about her feelings or not. Despite her claims, she was too good an actress, at least when it came to guarding her heart.

But then, she'd always been cautious, slow to trust. Perhaps that was why he'd been so sure their breakup had hurt her. Perhaps that was why he now believed she was lying about something. What, he wasn't sure. But he'd find out.

Five

"Okay," Cece murmured as she finished up her notes describing the Parisian cabaret where Lillian had been singing when she and Charles had first met. "Do you remember the names of any of the songs you sang?"

Lillian smiled, her gaze focused on something only she could see. After a moment, she looked back at Cece. "Ah. Of course I do." She hummed a few notes. "I remember them as if it was yesterday. *Comme moi* was always my favorite. But Charles preferred *Mon Homme*."

Cece quickly jotted down the names. She'd have to remember to bring her digital recorder next time she met with Lillian. Rereading her own handwritten notes helped her remember her feelings and impressions from an interview, but a recording was more helpful with facts, names and dates.

"Charles once told me that the first time he heard me sing *Mon Homme* was the moment he knew he was going to marry me."

Lillian's voice brimmed with love as she reminisced, but Cece felt the underlying sorrow behind Lillian's memories. Charles had been the love of her life. They'd had so many wonderful years together, until Charles had passed away fourteen years ago.

A strong woman, Lillian carried on, but with Charles's death a part of her had died as well. Their love had been at the center of their life. At the center of their whole family. Everyone had felt the loss.

Overcoming her own sadness, Cece looked up from her notes. The faint shimmer of tears didn't surprise her, but Lillian's lovely face seemed lined as it hadn't just a few hours ago when they'd started. The fragile skin under her eyes had darkened with exhaustion. There was even a faint tremble in her hands as she patted at her hair.

"You know, I think I have enough for today." Cece stood and stretched. "Why don't we stop right there?"

Lillian smiled with relief, but still asked, "Are you sure?"

"Absolutely. Besides, I should go check on Theo. We'll start up tomorrow morning. If that's okay with you?"

"Yes, dear. After breakfast, if you don't mind."

A few minutes later, after getting Lillian settled, Cece dropped her notebook back in her room before going in search of Theo. She knew Maria had planned on taking him swimming that afternoon, so Cece quickly changed into her black one-piece. She threw on a linen shirt over the suit and grabbed a towel.

However, when she made it to the pool, Maria wasn't with Theo. Jack was.

They stood together at the shallow end. Theo on one of the steps, Jack holding out his arms, waiting for Theo to jump off the step. Theo's arms were encased in his blow-up water wings.

Jack wore board shorts, long and loose, but snug enough

at the waist to accent his slim hips. His chest was blessedly bare, his muscles smooth and lightly tanned.

The sheer masculine beauty of his naked torso banished any hope she'd held that he'd gotten fat and flabby in the years since she'd last seen him naked. Nope, he was still knee-weakeningly delicious. Dang it.

And if it wasn't bad enough that he looked so blasted good, there he was, bonding with her son. Their son. Double dang it.

Kind of made her wish she hadn't sworn off all the bad curse words.

Jack's and Theo's attention was riveted on each other, so neither noticed her approaching. She refused to entertain the guilt rising in her gut over the sight of them together, choosing instead to focus on her irritation. The two of them getting along was the last thing she wanted.

She walked to within earshot.

"Come on, Teddyboy. You can do it."

Teddyboy? She didn't think so.

The only thing reassuring about the tableau before her was her certain knowledge that Jack would be thwarted in his attempts to get Theo off the step and into deeper waters. She took Theo swimming almost daily in their neighbor's pool. Though he adored the water and loved being held, he screamed the moment she stepped more than a foot or so away.

Jack might look great in swim trunks, but she knew her son.

Cece crossed her arms over her chest prepared to wait patiently for Theo to scream bloody murder. Whatever game Jack thought he was playing was sure to come to a screeching halt once Theo had pierced his eardrums.

Jack held up his hands, palms out, in a universal halt position. "On the count of three."

Cece sucked in a breath, poised to rush to her son's side.

"One." Jack began to inch back.

Okay, any second now.

"Two."

Theo—giggling with delight—hadn't yet noticed that Jack was backing away.

"Three."

Cece cringed, squeezed her eyes closed and waited for the bloodcurdling scream…that never came.

More giggling. A triumphant splash.

Her eyes popped open just in time to see Theo bobbed back to the surface in Jack's arms. Jack spun around, his arms full of wiggly kid.

"Again! Again!" Theo shouted.

"Okay, one more time. This time I'm going farther back."

Shock and betrayal washed over her, colder and more brutal than a splash of icy pool water in mid-January. Her baby—her Theo!—after a solid of year of coaxing on her part had finally jumped off the pool step. Not into her arms, but into Jack's.

Stalking across the patio, she wanted to launch herself into the pool and snatch Theo from Jack's grasp. "What's going on?"

Her tone sounded sharp, her words harsh.

Theo, all childish exuberance, didn't notice. "Swim, Mommy! I swimming!"

Jack had the good sense to pick up on her mood. "Uh-oh, Teddyboy, we've been caught."

"Caught? So you knew I wouldn't approve?"

"I swimming, Mommy!" Theo repeated, his pure joy making her feel like a shrew.

She forced a tight smile. "I see, Theo. Mommy's so proud."

Carrying Theo in his arms, Jack climbed the steps of the pool. He bundled Theo in a pool towel and steered him toward the house. "Why don't you go to the kitchen to see if Hannah has your snack ready yet?"

"Swim, swim, swim, swim," Theo chanted, taking exaggerated bouncy steps across the patio. Landing heavily with each word, he was blissfully unaware of her careening emotions.

"Where's Maria?" she asked, turning her wrath back on Jack.

"She got a call from the school. Her kid was sick."

"Why didn't she come get me?"

"Because I asked her not to. I know Lillian likes to rest in the afternoons and that you didn't have much longer to work. I was here and told her I'd take Theo for a couple of hours until you finished."

She opened her mouth, prepared to argue. When nothing more rational came to mind, she snapped, "So you're back to calling him Theo? So you do know what his real name is?"

Jack looked at her like she'd gone bonkers as he grabbed a towel from one of the lounge chairs and gave his chest a quick rub dry. "Come on, Cece. You can't seriously be mad that I called him Teddyboy."

"And took him swimming without my permission." But her protest sounded lame even to her. The anger fizzled out of her voice, leaving her feeling ridiculous.

She had way overreacted. Besides which, she should be glad they were spending time together. Her selfish and rash decision had deprived Theo of a father. If he could enjoy his father's attention for just a few short hours, shouldn't she be thankful? Logic said yes, but her fearful heart screamed in protest.

"Why don't you tell me what this is really about?" His tone was more chiding than scolding, but she still felt like a recalcitrant child.

He'd swung the towel around his neck and stood holding the ends of the towel in either hand, which emphasized both the breadth of his shoulders and the narrowness of his hips. She turned away to keep from staring at him. And—who was she kidding—to avoid his questioning gaze.

"Cece…" he prodded.

"I'm just…" Gosh, for a writer, she sure was having trouble putting her feelings into words. But dang it, this was a complicated situation. "Jealous, I guess. He doesn't do that for me."

But he didn't let her retreat. With gentle hands on her shoulders, he turned her back to face him and nudged her chin up. "Doesn't do what?"

There was genuine concern in his gaze, which only made her admission seem more ridiculous. "Jump off the step."

Jack chuckled. Not meanly, but with tender amusement. "All this drama because he jumped off the pool step for me?"

"It's not as silly as you're making it sound."

"Of course it is. As freaked out as you sounded, I expected his life to be in danger at least." Jack's eyes sparkled as he teased her. "I thought for sure Theo would melt into a puddle of goo from being in the water or something like that."

She couldn't help but laugh at the image. "Okay, so I overreacted a little."

"A little?"

She slanted him a dirty look. "Any chance you're going to let this go?"

"Nope. Not a chance." He swung a casual arm over her shoulder. "Let's go get some of that lemonade Hannah made."

Ignoring the heat his touch stirred up, she walked along beside him, pretending his bare chest wasn't brushing against her arm. Pretending his torso wasn't that enticingly cool from being in the water. Pretending she couldn't smell the faint hint of his woodsy soap lingering on his sun-warmed skin.

To distract herself, she wiggled out from under his arm and said, "I didn't overreact that much."

"I'm sure you didn't." His tone said he was humoring her. "I'm sure it was very traumatic. After all, what do I know? I'm not a parent."

His words sliced through her gut like a butcher knife.

She stumbled, but he didn't notice. Catching herself, she

stood stock-still, watching him walk toward the house. He made it only a few steps before turning and asking, his expression suddenly serious, "Hey, you okay?"

"Yeah. Sure." She caught up with him, but couldn't knock the sense that her earlier emotional swing was fueled as much by guilt and fear as by motherly instincts. She hadn't been upset that Theo would jump to someone else. She'd been upset that he jumped to Jack.

It seemed somehow a harbinger of things to come. A foreboding sign of a deeper bond they shared. As if Theo already knew on a subconscious level that Jack was his father. As if Theo were already choosing Jack over her.

And it would just be ridiculously unfair if Jack ended up with her heart and her son.

INT. CASINO DE MARSEILLES, NIGHT

CHARLES slips through the front door into the smoky, dimly lit club. From beyond the door come the sounds of soldiers on the street. He blends quickly into the crowd of French citizens and German soldiers. The band can barely be heard playing *Comme Moi* over the drunken carousing of the crowd. LILLIAN walks onto the stage.

LILLIAN
...Le rideau de soie bleue
Comme moi...

As she sings, LILLIAN parades down the steps into the crowd. Trailing her hand across the shoulder of GENERAL...

Cece stopped, hands poised over the keyboard. After a good thirty seconds, she clenched her fists. "Dang it. What was his name?"

She glanced down at the open notebook, then flipped

forward a few pages and then back a few. "Something with a *G*," she murmured. "General…what? Dang it."

The temptation was strong to bang her head against the wooden desk in the third-floor sitting room she'd commandeered as her office. Instead she popped a cinnamon Altoid in her mouth and munched for a minute. Nothing came to her.

She stood, knowing she could write on without it. Knowing she *should* write on without the name of General Whatever. Jeez, she could write the scene calling him General Bugs Bunny and no one would know the difference as long as she went back and fixed it later.

She glanced at the phone sitting on the desk. For that matter, she could call Lillian and ask. Hannah had mentioned just the other day that Lillian now carried her cell phone in her pocket, that way she could easily get ahold of Hannah if she needed her. Cece had jotted down the number in her notebook, so calling Lillian would be a simple enough matter and would save her the trip downstairs.

Still, she just couldn't make herself sit back down. Instead, she'd go ask Lillian. Lillian, she knew, wouldn't mind the interruption. It was just after lunch and Lillian would be watching her soap, a daily habit Cece remembered from the summers she spent at Hudson Manor all those years ago.

But as Cece headed for the door, she couldn't resist a quick glance out the window. The sitting room overlooked the back of the house. And the pool.

Just as she'd suspected, Jack and Theo were down at the pool. A stack of towels and T-shirts lay on the lounge chair beside the pool. Theo had started demanding he get to wear his own toddler board shorts that were similar to the swim trunks Jack wore. Even from this distance, they were clearly visible, their inky hair nearly identical in color, Jack's bare chest gleaming in the sun. Theo's paler skin bright against the cerulean blue of the water.

Maria hadn't been back since the day last week when she'd been called away. Her daughter had scarlet fever, which was far too contagious for her to be around Theo for at least a couple of weeks.

With Maria out of the picture, the task of caring for Theo had largely fallen on Hannah, who swore she didn't mind a bit. However, Jack had come by every afternoon to give Hannah a break and take Theo swimming. It was a system that allowed Cece to continue her grueling work schedule, even if it did make her uncomfortable.

Surely—she had protested—studio executives had better things to do with their time than babysit. Her protestations had fallen on deaf ears. Right now—Jack had countered—his highest priority was making sure she did her job.

The logic didn't comfort her. No matter how much sense it made, she didn't like how much time Jack and Theo were spending together. Yes, she was jealous. But it was more than that. If Jack and Theo did become close, Jack would just shut down the relationship, the way he always did. After all, that was what he'd done to her.

But of course, that was only the tip of the iceberg. Theo and Jack simply looked too much alike. Sooner or later, Jack would notice that Theo's hair was the same color as his. Or that Theo had Jack's smile, crooked and a little rueful, even at two. Not to mention the legendary Hudson blue eyes. Eyes that sometimes seemed a pale, icy blue and other times seemed to darken with intense emotion.

He wasn't an idiot. Eventually he'd notice the truth. The fact that he hadn't yet made her wonder if he was being willfully dense. If he hadn't subconsciously figured it out and was just ignoring the truth because he didn't want to be a father. Or maybe she just wanted to believe that because it made her lie easier to stomach. Either way she could come up with only so many excuses to keep them apart.

For now she was reduced to watching and worrying. And pointless procrastination. Fretting over Jack and Theo's growing bond was pointless. She could do nothing to prevent it. The more she protested the time they spent together, the more suspicious Jack would become. She should really just keep her mouth shut and get back to work.

But since she was up already, she might as well go downstairs and ask Lillian the name of that general, the one she'd been trying to seduce for information.

Cece grabbed her notebook and headed for the staircase. She'd stop by Lillian's room, ask a few quick questions and come back upstairs. She would not go outside to check on Theo. Probably.

Her internal debate followed her down the stairs and through the first floor all the way to Lillian's sitting room. Grateful for the distraction, she rapped lightly on the door before entering the room.

"Sorry to interrupt your soap, Lillian, but—" she broke off sharply when she looked down.

Lillian lay crumpled on the floor beside her favorite wingback chair.

Cece's heart jumped into her throat. Dropping her notebook she rushed across the room and knelt beside Lillian.

"Oh, God," she murmured, pressing her fingertips to Lillian's neck, desperate to find a pulse. Her throat seemed to close around her words. "Please be all right. Please."

After a moment she fumbled for Lillian's pocket and found

the cell phone tucked inside. Her fingers trembled as she dialed 911.

"We need an ambulance at Hudson Manor, Loma Vista Drive in Beverly Hills."

Six

Jack couldn't imagine how he'd have made it through the day without Cece by his side. Since he was the only family member at the house, he'd ridden in the ambulance alongside Lillian. Though the EMT had been able to wake her and she'd protested fiercely against the need for a trip to the hospital, no one wanted to take any chances. In the end, it was Cece's quiet, no-nonsense insistence that had convinced Lillian it wouldn't hurt to be checked out.

A tearful Hannah had agreed to stay at the house with Theo while Cece had driven Jack's car to the hospital, arriving just moments after he had. It had taken hours for the emergency room doctors to see her and decide a course of action. By the time Lillian had been admitted to the hospital and moved to a room, Cece had already completed the arduous task of calling all the Hudsons and letting them know the bad news. With the exception of Sabrina and Bella, who'd been out shopping, they had all been at the studio, which meant driving across town in what was now rush-hour traffic. Now, it was merely a matter of waiting for Lillian to be seen by her own doctor and waiting for people to start showing up.

As if she'd sensed his growing impatience, Cece had even sent Jack down to get them coffee from the Starbucks in the South Tower. By the time he returned, she was creeping out of Lillian's room, closing the door behind her.

She said, "She just drifted off."

"Has the doctor been by yet?"

"Actually, yes. But she made me wait in the hall while he talked to her. And then he wouldn't tell me anything other than she's stable, which—jeez—the EMTs were able to tell us." She rolled her eyes in obvious annoyance. "I tried playing the goddaughter card, but he didn't buy it. Said he needed to talk to someone in the family. He swears he'll be back by in a few minutes."

He extended the cup toward her and she took it from him.

"You seem to always be bringing me coffee." She sipped, casting him a rueful glance. "Thank goodness you remember how I take it."

He appreciated the attempt at humor, no matter how lame. The initial panic and fear had faded into a sort of rotelike efficiency, but he felt the lingering effects of the stress still filtering through his body like dangerous toxins. Like a bad hangover, stress all but seeped through his pores.

Still he couldn't let her self-deprecating comment pass. Lillian's collapse was an all-too-vivid reminder of how few people he had in his life who cared about him. Suddenly he couldn't remember why he'd been trying so hard to push Cece away.

"Do you really think I'd forget?" With his free hand he

reached to brush aside an errant lock of her hair. "Do you really think I've forgotten one minute of our time together?"

Her eyes seemed to widen with intensity as she swayed toward him. For a moment the lines of worry faded.

Then she shook her head. Stepping back to put distance between them, she took another sip of her coffee.

"What I believe, Jack, is that you have charm to spare and more audacity than sense when it comes to women. What I *can't* believe is that you'd try to put moves on me while we're standing outside your grandmother's hospital room."

"Is that what you really think of me?"

"What am I supposed to think?"

He stared at her blankly, unsure how to respond.

"You know what I've learned about men in the years we've been apart, Jack? Men basically have two emotions. Anger and desire and they're afraid to express anything else." She shook her head with a cynical chuckle. "So maybe that means I shouldn't be surprised. You're worried sick about Lillian, but you don't want to face the fact that she's almost ninety years old, that we could lose her. If not today, then soon. That even if this turns out to be nothing, she's still getting older and just won't be around forever." She reached up and cupped his cheek with her hand, her expression somehow both sad and comforting. "You don't want to deal with how that makes you feel. So instead you're hitting on me, because it's so much easier to feel desire than sorrow."

Annoyance brushed over the attraction he'd felt just moments ago. Oh, he still wanted her, but now his desire had a sharp edge to it. "I guess you think you've got me all figured out."

She shook her head, her eyes wide with mock innocence. "I'd never presume to say that."

"But—once again—you'd presume to tell me how I feel."

"I suppose you're going to tell me I've got it all wrong?"

Her smug confidence rankled. Her sassy mouth had always been a large part of her appeal. But he liked it better when it wasn't aimed toward him.

He reached out and snaked a hand around her wrist. He tugged her toward him, pulling her off balance, so she fell against his chest. He freed her wrist only to bracket the back of her head, effectively trapping her lips mere inches from his.

The utilitarian surroundings only heightened the tension between them. Somewhere in the ward, an orderly was making rounds, pushing a cart with rattling wheels. Over that arrhythmic stuttering, Jack could just barely hear Cece's breathing. He could tell that her heart was just beginning to beat faster. Just as his was.

"Maybe you're right," he said. "Maybe I am trying not to think about Lillian and whether or not she's sick. But that doesn't mean I don't want you. And at least I'm not trying to pretend there's nothing between us."

Her lips parted as she drew in a deep breath. Suddenly he was struck by the memory of what it had been like to kiss her. How her lips had always been soft and moist. How she'd always tasted vaguely of surprise, as if she never expected him to kiss her. And as if she never expected him to kiss her again.

And cinnamon. She ate cinnamon Altoids when she wrote, and the flavor always lingered.

No other woman tasted like that. No other lips felt like that. No other kiss made him feel what hers had. Her touch had made the world disappear. Had made him feel as if they were the only two people. As if her love were all he needed, all he'd ever need. He had it all in his grasp and he'd let it go.

He felt a sudden, desperate urge to kiss her. To feel that again.

Maybe she was right. Maybe he was just sublimating his

concern about Lillian. Was there any other explanation for this desire?

He tipped her chin up and caught the faint whiff of cinnamon as she exhaled and he lowered his mouth to hers.

Jack hadn't kissed her. She'd been waiting for it—wanting it, even—when he released her and stepped away. The damn tease.

The fact that Max Hudson, Jack's cousin, was walking down the hall didn't make Jack's sudden withdrawal feel any less like a kick in the teeth. In fact, it almost made it worse. As Max approached, she couldn't miss the gleam of curiosity, and maybe even censure in his gaze. Which meant she felt cheap in addition to feeling rejected. Perfect. Maybe she'd glance down and find out she'd forgotten to put pants on this morning and realize this was all just some demented bad dream.

"Cece." Max gave her a brusque nod.

From his tone, she sensed he wasn't pleased to see her. Whether that was because he'd nearly caught her and Jack kissing—behavior that was hardly kosher under circumstances such as these—or because he didn't think she had the right to be here, Cece couldn't guess. Either implication was unpleasant. And just *so* not what she needed at the moment.

"Cece's the one who found Lillian," Jack explained. "If she hadn't checked in on her, who knows how long it would have been before Lillian was found."

Feeling suitably mortified she slunk off to the nurses' station to hunt down the doctor. When she didn't have any luck, she returned just as Dev and Markus, Jack's cousin and uncle, were rounding the corner. Bella, the youngest of the Hudson cousins, and her mother, Sabrina, showed up a few minutes after that. For once Bella didn't have her dog, Muffin, with her. Cece couldn't imagine what she'd done with the dog, which she'd probably brought on the shopping trip, but obviously he hadn't been allowed into the hospital with her. Luc and his new fiancée, Gwen McCord, walked up a moment later.

Only Charlotte was missing. But then, she'd been raised abroad by her maternal grandparents. Now, she served as hostess for her grandfather, who was the ambassador to Monte Allegre. Although Cece had left a message on Charlotte's voice mail, the other woman was no doubt still abroad. Cece hadn't even tried to reach David, Jack's father, having recently read that he was finishing up post-production on a movie in Prague.

They were a tight-knit, recalcitrant group, these Hudsons. She'd practically grown up among them and still she felt the walls they'd built to protect the family from the rest of the world. It must come, she realized, from being part of such a powerful family. The Hudsons were the last of the true Hollywood dynasties. They were the closest thing America had to royalty. By comparison, her own showbiz heritage was practically blue-collar, rather than blue blood.

She stood just off to the side, painfully aware of the tight little circle they'd formed as they spoke in the hall. All the men wore suits. Even Jack had quickly changed back into his while waiting for the ambulance to arrive, his missing tie and belt a testament to the speed with which he'd dressed. Bella and Sabrina were both dressed with the casual elegance typical of a shopping trip to Rodeo Drive. The only outsider they'd allowed in was Gwen, who stood with Luc's arm possessively about her waist, her head resting on his shoulder.

"When did she get to the hospital?"

"Do we know anything more?"

"Has anybody spoken to her doctor yet?"

Jack answered each question in turn. And just when Cece was wondering if she could quietly slip away, the doctor reappeared. Since she was the one he'd spoken to earlier, he approached her first, apparently not noticing the looks of annoyance this earned him.

With a pointed look at the nearby bustling nurses' station, Jack said, "Maybe we can discuss this in Lillian's room."

Cece tried to hang back, but Jack slipped an arm around her waist and pulled her along into the room before him. They quickly filed into Lillian's room, huddling in the narrow alcove formed by the privacy curtain just inside the door.

Dr. Greenburg, a portly man with a graying beard who could probably moonlight as a mall Santa, stood with his hands folded behind his back, rocking backward and forward on his heels, seemingly unaware of the verbal firing squad he was about to face.

"I'm sure you have a lot of questions," he began.

"What can you tell us?" Max asked.

"Not much until Lillian wakes," Dr. Greenburg stated baldly. "She's stable for now."

"Why is she here?" Bella asked.

"Well…" Dr. Greenburg frowned. "As I understand it, she collapsed at home and—"

"No, I understand why she's in the hospital," Bella interrupted. "I mean, once she was admitted, why did they bring her here to the Breast Cancer Center?"

Bella's question seemed to hang in the air, the word *cancer* stunning them all into silence. All the Hudsons, Cece noticed, looked as if they'd been hit by two-by-fours. Which was about how she felt as well.

For her part, Bella looked pointedly at her brothers and cousin, eyebrows raised. "Did anyone else notice the sign when you got off the elevator?"

Several people looked at Cece. "I…" She shrugged in confusion. "I didn't notice it. I had no idea what was on this floor. In the emergency room, they told me she'd been admitted to room 506, so that's where I told people to come."

As she spoke she was acutely aware of Jack's hand on her waist. Of the force of his grip, both reassuring and clutching. As if he needed her there to anchor him.

Jack turned to the doctor. "Is this true? Is she here because she has breast cancer?"

Dr. Greenburg held firm to doctor-patient confidentiality. "I'm afraid I can't say anything more."

His words roused a round of protests from the Hudsons. The air seemed to have left the room and Cece wasn't sure if it was because Jack's grip was squeezing all the air out of her lungs or because her growing dread had stolen it.

Dr. Greenburg compressed his lips, holding firm against the barrage of questions. Then a reedy voice broke through from the hospital room beyond the alcove.

"It's okay, Dr. Greenburg. It's time they knew."

Someone swept aside the curtain and as one, they turned to see Lillian, sitting up in bed, looking small and frail against the stark white of the sheets. Her eyes were weary, her skin wrinkled, her thin hands folded on top of the sheets.

She seemed to meet the gaze of each person in turn as she spoke. "I have breast cancer. I have less than a year to live."

Seven

She hadn't expected Jack to drive her home, but he had.

After Lillian had dropped her bombshell, Cece had assumed he'd stay at the hospital with his family. However, once things at the hospital calmed down, Jack had insisted on driving her back to Hudson Manor himself. When she tried again to sneak away—planning to call a cab to pick her up and bring her back to Hudson Manor—he extricated himself from the hushed and intense huddle that had formed after Lillian had ordered everyone from her room.

Since Jack had insisted on driving her home, she'd thought maybe he'd want to talk about Lillian, or the script at the very least. He hadn't. Instead he drove in stony silence, his face etched with unspoken grief, his shoulders taut with constrained tension. She was unsure what to say and even less sure that anything she could say would be welcomed.

She was a master at the witty repartee, but a disaster when

it came to sharing burdens and easing pain. It didn't help matters that her own heart felt heavy with loss.

How could Lillian be dying? Lillian, who seemed so lively and vibrant, even at her most frail. Lillian, who could still command a room with a single well-timed word. It was inconceivable that she was dying.

And yet somehow right, as well. Ever since Charles's death, Cece had had the feeling that Lillian was living on borrowed time. As if some part of her had passed with Charles and she was merely waiting to join him.

By the time Cece and Jack made it back to Hudson Manor, it was after ten. They found Theo asleep in front of the TV, Hannah by his side—asleep as well, with her head tipped back, snoring softly. They'd obviously fallen asleep watching a Disney flick because the movie had ended and the screen displayed the DVD's menu, the theme music caught in an annoying loop. Theo's head lay on Hannah's lap; her hand rested on his ruffled hair.

Cece turned off the TV and the DVD player, then dimmed the room's lights before going to pick up Theo. No point in risking waking him. When she turned around, she saw Jack gently shaking Hannah awake. A mother and grandmother herself, Hannah woke silently, ready to coax Theo back to sleep if need be.

Before Cece could cross back to the sofa to retrieve Theo, Jack had scooped the boy up in his arms. Theo's dark curls were matted and damp, as they often were when he slept; his lashes, long inky spikes against his cheeks. He moaned lightly when Jack lifted him into his arms, then nestled his cheek against Jack's chest, his lashes fluttering slightly as he fell into a deeper sleep.

Only then did she notice that Theo—instead of getting

dressed in his own clothes after swimming—had put on the dusky blue T-shirt Jack had worn earlier in the day.

Hannah must have noticed Cece looking at the shirt, because as she stood, she gave a little shrug and said, "He insisted on wearing it. I couldn't talk him out of it, no matter what I said. I think he sensed something was wrong and that was just his way of dealing with his worries."

A question hung unasked at the end of her statement. Jack sent Cece a shuttered look, and she knew automatically he wasn't up to filling in Hannah.

But as she watched Jack and Theo leave the room, she felt her heart tighten. The T-shirt enveloped Theo's tiny frame, yet somehow it looked right. Endearing, maybe. He looked good in his father's T-shirt. He looked good in his father's arms.

Cece explained things to Hannah quickly, knowing the other woman wouldn't want anything sugarcoated. Hannah nodded, her hands knotted tightly before her, her eyes welling with tears as she heard the news.

"I suspected it might be something like this," Hannah tsked. "Lillian never was one to ask for help when she needed it. She always preferred to downplay the bad."

Still, despite Hannah's obvious distress, she moved about the room, tidying things up with the brusque efficiency Cece had come to expect of her.

A moment later Hannah said, "I'd best be getting to my own bed. Goodness knows there'll be plenty to do in the morning to keep me busy. Is someone staying with her tonight?"

"Markus is staying at the hospital overnight. Sabrina will sit with her in the morning," Cece said.

A moment later, Cece trudged up the stairs, partly glad she didn't have to carry Theo's thirty pounds of weight, yet somehow missing the reassuring feeling of his sturdy body pressed against hers.

To give them as much privacy as possible, Hannah had given them rooms at the far end of the hall. When she reached the room she and Theo had been staying in, she found Jack waiting outside the door.

"I wasn't sure which room was Theo's. The yellow bedroom seemed to be the only one being used, so I put him in there on the bed."

"That's fine. He's had trouble adjusting to being in such a big house, so he's been sleeping in the bed with me."

Jack nodded his understanding, but his expression remained distant. As if he were only half there. Only half participating in the conversation. Of course, if that were the case, who could blame him?

The day had been long and hard on everyone and as much as she ached to slip into the oblivion of sleep, she didn't want to just leave Jack standing out here alone. So when he headed back down the hall toward the staircase, she fell into step beside him.

After a moment, he spoke. "I don't know what I would have done without you today."

His expression was stark, his posture defensive from taking so many emotional blows. Some people shrank into their grief as if overwhelmed by it. Jack didn't. Instead he seemed to expand to fill it. As if pain somehow increased his body mass.

Unsure what else to say, she settled for go-for-broke honesty. "I'm not good at this emotional stuff, Jack. You know me, when you're ready for sarcastic quips and snappy dialogue, I'm your girl. But for this? I'm drawing a blank. I'm sure there are plenty of women who know just what to say that would make you feel better, that would help you find peace about this, but I'm not that person. I wish I was. But I'm not."

He stopped and turned to search her face. For the first time since they'd heard the news, he seemed to shake off his shock. To be present in the moment. And it was then that she realized how close she stood to him. The dimly lit quiet of the hallway reinforced the feeling of intimacy that grief had knitted around them.

They'd stopped maybe fifty feet from the room she and Theo shared. Empty rooms lined the hall on either side of them, but still he whispered when he spoke. Cupping her chin, he said, "You're right. I do know you. And I don't expect any worthless platitudes from you. I don't want you to be anything other than what you are. You're brutally honest. It's one of your better qualities. And let's face it, there's nothing anyone could say right now that would make this better."

His hand was warm against her cheek. His palm rough, but his touch gentle.

"No, I suppose there isn't," she agreed.

"Lillian's dying. It doesn't matter that—"

His voice broke and he seemed unable to go on.

Seeing him like this—seeing Jack, who always knew the right thing to say, at a loss for words—was almost too much for her. So she wrapped her arms around his waist and did the only thing she knew to do. She held him.

She cradled him in her arms and held on tight. As if her embrace could hold at bay all the sorrow they both knew waited in their future.

His body felt warm and hard against her. The heat that seemed to course between them was a real and vibrant thing; not just comfort and solace, but desire as well. After a moment, he pulled back far enough to cradle her face in his hands and lower his mouth to hers. This time, there was no family to interrupt them. Nothing to intrude.

It didn't surprise her how quickly the hug that she'd meant to provide as comfort turned to something more. What surprised her was how little resistance she had to his kiss.

She knew better than to want him. After all, he'd broken her heart before. His desertion had crushed her. And everything she'd said at the hospital was still true. He was grieving. But men didn't feel grief. They channeled it into lust, which meant all the desire on his end was an illusion.

She *knew* that. Intellectually at least.

But when Jack kissed her, her intellect flew out the window. Her body took over. And her body wanted his. It craved the sweet release she'd found only when his mouth sought her breasts. When his fingers caressed the deepest, secret parts of her body. When his body pounded into hers.

His kiss was a precursor to all of that. Both firm and gentle, persuasive but unrelenting. His tongue stroked hers, sending fissures of pleasure deep into her stomach. She felt herself melt against him, relishing the strength of his body, the hardened muscles. The very height and breadth of him.

Desire coiled through her, hot and needy. Like a living entity, separate from herself and over which she had no control.

It had been too long, far too long, since she'd been with a man. When Jack cupped her buttocks and pulled her tight to him, she relished the sensation of his erection against the V between her legs. He was hard to her softness. A moment of release to her growing desire.

Her hand clutched at his shirt, fumbling with his buttons.

He pulled back and his lips quirked into a smile. "Trying to undress me?"

Despite his smile, sorrow haunted his eyes. She knew instantly what he was doing. He wanted, just for a few moments, to push aside his grief. To play. To forget that the woman who'd been the one constant in his tumultuous life was dying.

Since she wanted that, too, she took her cue from him. Grief could overwhelm them both or together they could hold it at bay just a little bit longer. With a playfulness she didn't feel, she tugged on his hand, pulling him down the hall, farther away from the bedroom she'd been sharing with Theo. When she found a spare room, she drew him inside, shutting the door behind them as she asked, "Why? Do you want to make sure all those times you flaunted your bare chest out by the pool has paid off?"

As she spoke, she pulled each of his shirt buttons free, rubbing her hands over his chest as she revealed it to her touch.

"Flaunting? If anyone was flaunting, it was you. Prancing around in that swimsuit of yours." He rained nibbling kisses down her neck to her collarbone. He groaned.

"My black one-piece?"

"Yes."

"Are we talking about the same suit?"

"You don't know how many times I wanted to rip it off your body."

As he spoke, his hand crept up under her shirt. With a rapid flicker of his fingers, her bra came unhooked. Her whole body trembled with anticipation as she waited for his hand to reach her bare breast. And she had to stifle a groan of her own.

"And here I thought it was very demure," she commented with as much innocence as she could muster. Which was hard when unbuckling a man's belt.

"Yes. That damn thing. You can't imagine how tempting a swimsuit is when it covers that much of your body."

She eyed his shirt and pants. "Oh, I can imagine."

His fingers found her nipples, tweaking them to hard pebbles, making her ache and shudder. Her breath caught, coming in rapid pants. She wanted to close her eyes. To lose herself in the sensation. To simply let her aching need sweep her away. But, dang it, if he could talk, so could she.

"If I'd known I was providing such temptation, I would have picked out a bikini."

"You wouldn't dare." He backed her up against the wall, pressing his body against hers.

She retaliated by running her fingers down the length of his erection. Anticipation rocketed through her as she felt his body clench and shudder in response.

He grabbed her hand and his gaze met hers, suddenly serious, his eyes dark with passion and searing with intensity. "You should stop now."

She didn't want what he was offering. The chance to change her mind. The moment of logic and reason to think things through. To be responsible.

She had enough of that in her everyday life. Enough responsibility. Enough logic. Enough common sense. What she wanted now was searing mindlessness. Blind passion. Forgetfulness.

So she wrapped her fingers around the length of him and smiled. "Stop? What are you going to do, make me?"

He nodded and there was only a faint glimmer of sadness in his eyes, a silent acknowledgment of what they were both doing—holding their sorrow at bay. Then he grinned and reached for the snap on her jeans. "Don't say I didn't warn you."

She nearly groaned with frustration when he released her, until she realized he was reaching into his back pocket, fumbling for his wallet. She shimmied out of her jeans and panties. A moment later his wallet dropped to the floor and he held up the condom.

"Score one for the Boy Scouts," she murmured appreciatively.

"Hey I'm not always this prepared. This time I got lucky."

"I'd say we're both about to get lucky."

His fingers sought and stroked the folds of her desire.

She squeezed her eyes closed, clutching his shoulders as first one leg and then the other snaked up off the floor to wrap around his hips. And then he was pressing into her. So deeply and so fully that she had no room for thought or pain or grief.

Or regrets.

Only for him. For this passion. For the one thing they'd always gotten right.

He'd planned to leave Cece sleeping in bed early in the morning. They'd slept in the bed in the elegantly appointed guest room, where they'd made love a second time before falling asleep. It seemed a simple enough prospect to sneak out before dawn. After all, he knew better than anyone that she was a late sleeper.

However, in the end, she was the one to wake him as she silently gathered up her clothes from the bedroom floor. Only the faintest hint of light shone through the open door to illuminate her form as she dressed.

"Cece?"

She started guiltily, a sure sign she hadn't meant to wake him. "Hi, Jack."

"You're sneaking out."

"I need to be back in my room when Theo wakes up."

"You weren't going to wake me up before leaving, were you?" He sat up, the sheet falling to his waist.

She didn't even bother to look guilty at his accusation. She merely shrugged. "Come on, Jack, let's not make more of this than it is. Old habits die hard. Under the circumstances, it's not surprising something like this happened."

"Old habits die hard?" Bitterness tinged his voice. He ran a hand through his hair, scraping his nails against the back of his head. "And here I thought this was consolation sex. How many excuses do you think you need to sleep with me?"

"You think these are excuses to sleep with you?" She tugged her T-shirt over her head. "Well, they're not. They're reasons not to get involved with you again."

The absolute conviction of her words stung. "I don't recall asking you to get involved."

"Oh, no," she scoffed, tugging on her jeans with brusque motions. "Of course you wouldn't want to 'get involved' with me." She made bunny ears with her fingers at the words *get involved.* "That would be way too much commitment for you."

He didn't bother to pretend he didn't know what she meant. After all, she was right. Commitment just wasn't his thing. He wouldn't wish himself on anyone, let alone someone he cared about.

When he didn't answer, her expression soured. Amazing how she managed to look both lovely and pissed off.

She yanked on the zipper of her jeans and rammed her feet into her shoes. "You haven't changed one bit."

She strayed close enough to the bed that he reached out to grab her wrist. He tugged her toward him and she lost her balance, tumbling onto the bed. Rolling, he trapped her under him.

"No. I haven't changed. And neither has this attraction between us. All I want is for you to admit it." She bucked against him and a spark of sexual awareness lit her eyes. But her defiance was equally strong as she boldly met his gaze. "Just admit it," he goaded.

"I don't understand what you're talking about." She enunciated each word with slow defiance.

"It's not like you to ignore the truth. You've always been one of the most honest people I've ever known."

She blanched, then pulled away from him with such ferocity he had little choice but to let her go. She snatched her shoes off the ground on her way to the door. He expected her to storm out of the room, but at the last minute, she spun back around.

"You want honesty? Here it is. I have a son. My life is complicated in ways you can't imagine."

"Oh, I get that you have a son. I've been spending quite a bit of time with him lately."

"Trust me. Being a parent is more than spending a couple of afternoons swimming with a kid at the pool."

He swung his legs over the side of the bed. "Yeah. I get that."

She shook her head. "Obviously you don't. And even if you do, it's a moot point. Face it, Jack, you dodge responsibility."

He scanned the floor for his own jeans and, spotting them, crossed to snatch them up off the floor. "I'm an executive of a major company. I'm responsible for movies, careers and hundreds of millions of dollars. I'm not some slacker."

Her hand seemed to spasm on the shoe she held in her hand and for a second he thought she might throw it at him. "You've been in the industry since you were in diapers. Obviously, you excel at that. I'm not talking about your job. I'm talking about your personal life. When we were together—"

"We were great together."

"Sure. For about a minute. And then you did what you always do in relationships. As soon as you thought I was getting serious, you pulled away. Next thing I know I'm in the checkout lane seeing pictures of you with some hot starlet."

"I never slept with her."

"It doesn't matter whether or not you slept with her. If you cared about me at all you wouldn't have been seen with her in the first place. You were trying to make me miserable so that I'd end the relationship. And you know what, it worked. You won."

He clenched his jaw and shoved his hand into his pocket, trying to bury the anger her words stirred up. "I'm glad you think you know me so well."

"I don't *think* I know you. I know I do. You didn't want the responsibility of being in a real relationship when it was just me. You're sure as hell not going to want to be in one with me *and* my son."

She paused by the door, apparently waiting for him to stop her. But he didn't. How could he stop her from walking out of his life when that was exactly what he'd wanted her to do?

Eight

Cece shifted the strap to her laptop bag on her shoulder and knocked on the hospital room door. There was no answer, but she knew Lillian expected her, so she nudged the door open and peeked inside to see Lillian asleep.

Lillian had called just after breakfast and all but ordered Cece to visit her in the hospital around lunchtime. "I'm dying," she'd barked. "I'm not an invalid. Not yet, anyway. We've still got work to do, you and I. And I can do it just as well from my hospital bed as I can from my house."

Cece had been eager to escape Hudson Manor anyway, so she'd packed up her laptop, notebooks and digital recorder, left Theo in Hannah's care, and made the trek to the hospital. If she left now, merely because Lillian was napping, Cece knew the older woman would rake her over the coals.

Obviously Lillian was determined not to let her illness keep her from contributing to the making of *Honor*. She was more determined than ever to see the movie made by the studio's sixtieth anniversary. Undoubtedly the rest of the Hudsons would feel the same. Now the anniversary wasn't the only deadline they were working against. They needed to finish the movie while Lillian was still alive. It would be their final tribute to the great love Charles and Lillian had shared. The love on which Hudson Studios had been built. The very foundation of all of their lives.

As Cece stood in Lillian's hospital room, listening to the rhythmic beeping of her heart monitor and the shushing flow of her IV drip, her frailty was impossible to ignore. The enormous equipment dwarfed her delicate form.

Naturally, Lillian had been brought to the best hospital in the area. She'd been given the nicest room on the floor, one decorated more like an elegant hotel than a hospital room. However, an oak armoire and gilded wallpaper, no matter how refined, couldn't cover the ugly truth: This was the hospital room of a dying woman.

Cece would do everything in her power to fulfill Lillian's last request. This would be the best damn thing she'd ever written. It had to be. After creeping into the room, she lowered herself to the recliner beside the bed. She set her laptop bag on the floor beside the chair before pulling out her notebook and pen. There were notes she could take, scenes to plan out, lists to be made. Yet, she sat there, pen poised over the paper, waiting for something—anything—to write. Nothing made it to the paper except for a slowly growing ink splotch. She couldn't stop thinking about Jack.

After last night, part of her wanted to duck and run. Going to bed with him had been a huge mistake. And frankly, she had no excuse. Sure, Jack could explain away the moment of weakness—he was the one who'd been grieving. But what excuse did she have? Sure, she loved Lillian, too, but she wasn't family. Not really. All Cece would be losing was a beloved godmother, not the woman who'd raised her.

The only way Cece could explain her behavior was to chalk it up to pure sexual frustration. There had been no one since Jack. No one she'd wanted enough.

For a long time, she'd still been too in love with Jack. Things might have ended badly, but before that, when the relationship was going well…then, it had been great. Jack might be sexy beyond belief, but he was also funny and smart. He made her laugh. He was the best friend she'd ever had.

So, no. There had been no one else since him. Besides, she'd been pregnant. And then a new mother. She'd been too tired for that sort of thing. So there'd been no wild flings in Europe. No dating. Very little flirting and certainly no sex. Wild and passionate or otherwise. Because who could ever live up to that?

And now she saw what a mistake that had been. How vulnerable it had made her to Jack. She might have gotten over him, she might have moved on with her life, but she had never stopped loving him.

All this meant was she'd have to be more careful in the future. For obvious reasons, she couldn't simply cut him out of her life—much as she'd like to. Sleeping with him again was equally impossible—the risk to her heart was too great. Not to mention the risk of Jack discovering the truth about Theo.

In short, the situation could prove disastrous on all fronts. And there was no way she could extricate herself. Her only option—

"If you're going to sit there all afternoon just staring into space, we'll never get this script done."

Cece started nervously at the sound of Lillian's voice. "You caught me woolgathering," she admitted. Far better to say that than admit she'd been caught obsessing about Jack.

She flipped the notebook open to her page of questions,

then reached for her digital recorder. "But I'm ready to get to work now."

"Before we get started…"

Lillian's lightly accented voice sounded just as firm and strong as ever, only the faintest quiver hinting at the strain she was under.

Cece leaned forward and rested her hand on Lillian's. "I can come another time. If it's too much for—"

"Nonsense. I'm as strong as ever."

Cece quirked an eyebrow. "You don't have to pretend for me. I know you don't want anyone worrying about you. But I won't tell Jack—"

"My dear Cece, I'm very aware of the things you won't tell my grandson."

Dread crawled along her spine. "What do you mean?"

"I would think my meaning is obvious." Her tone held only a hint of reprimand. "Theo is Jack's son."

Cece felt all the blood drain from her face. Shocked, she sat back in her chair. "How did you know?"

"I knew the moment I met Theo. He looks just like Jack did at that age. All that curly black hair and those enormous blue eyes."

"I suspected they looked alike," Cece mused. "But it had been years since I'd seen a picture of Jack as a young child. I had no way of knowing."

"Frankly I'm surprised more people haven't figured it out. I suspected long before I even met Theo."

"You suspected?"

"Naturally. You adopted a baby in Europe?" Lillian waved a hand dismissively. "Don't forget I worked in the Golden Age of Hollywood when actresses had morality clauses that kept them from bearing children out of wedlock. Half the women I knew claimed to have adopted their children in Europe."

"And here I thought I was being original."

"Pshaw. When you're as old as I am, you'll realize there are no original ideas."

"But how did you—" Cece began.

"Know he was Jack's?" Lillian finished. "You think I don't own a calendar?"

"It's not that. I just didn't…" She trailed off, unsure exactly how to phrase it.

"Ah, you didn't think I knew about you two."

"Exactly." Cece fought against the blush creeping into her cheeks.

Despite Lillian's comments about morality clauses and the Golden Age of Hollywood, Cece felt vaguely ashamed that Lillian knew *she'd* had a child out of wedlock. Which was odd, because it wasn't something she was ashamed of. She honestly didn't feel she'd done anything wrong. Not telling Jack about Theo from the beginning…well, that was another matter entirely.

But Lillian was a woman who brought out the best in people, Cece concluded. Guilt burned through Cece at the thought of Lillian knowing not only about her indiscretion, but also about the lies she'd told.

"You must think I'm awful."

"No." Lillian spoke with firm conviction. "I think you must have been very afraid. And I think you're a brave woman to raise a child on your own. Goodness knows I couldn't have done it."

"You're being too easy on me." Suddenly relief swept through her, washing away the guilt and shame. Finally she had someone with whom she could discuss Theo's parentage.

Until now, only her mother had known the truth. Fresh from the recent divorce, Kate had taken a firm "screw the jerk" stance. Every time Cece wondered aloud if she should tell Jack, Kate had launched into another diatribe against men in general. Behavior that was hardly helpful.

But now there was at least one other person who knew the truth. Shaking her head, she released a chuckle that sounded both wry and sad. "I guess confession really is good for the soul. As awful as I feel about what I've done, at least now you know."

Lillian's gaze sharpened. "Which is why you must tell Jack the truth."

She recoiled, physically and emotionally. "I can't tell Jack."

Lillian reached out a hand, giving Cece no choice but to take it. Cece scooted to the very edge of her seat, extending her arms across the vast width of the hospital bed to reach and cradle Lillian's hand in her own. Her grasp felt weak, her hand as light as air. Lillian patted the back of Cece's hand.

"You must tell him," she repeated.

"Don't you see, I can't tell him. He'll be furious."

Lillian merely quirked an elegant eyebrow.

In that moment, she looked so much like Jack. Their features weren't all that similar, but sometimes their expressions of regal disdain were identical.

"Okay." She pulled her hands from Lillian's and had to resist knotting them together. "So he deserves to be angry."

"Indeed."

"But surely you see why I haven't told him." Even as she said the words, Cece was tempted to drop her head into her hands. She sounded so defensive. Throwing out one excuse after another, like a guilty defendant hoping for a reprieve. Still, she kept talking. "The last thing Jack wants is to be a father."

"He told you this?"

Annoyance flashed through Cece, both at Lillian and at herself. How dare Lillian be so logical? And why couldn't she have foreseen that Lillian would have asked exactly that question?

"No," she admitted. "He hasn't told me that. But then I haven't exactly had the perfect opportunity to ask him, either. It's not the kind of question you can subtly weave into conversation."

Of course, if she *was* going to weave a question like that into a conversation, the one she and Jack had had this morning would have been the perfect one. Not that she would admit *that* to Lillian.

Guiltily Cece added, "It just hasn't come up yet. But I know how he feels about this." She sighed, her own frustration with Jack seeping through. "When Jack and I were involved before, he made it abundantly clear that a committed relationship of any kind was the last thing he wanted."

Lillian frowned. "Yes. I know Jack has always thought marriage and a family aren't for him. And with his parents' relationship, it's no wonder." Regret lay heavy in her words. "I suppose Charles and I are to blame for that."

"You don't really believe that," Cece protested.

There was the faintest tremble in Lillian's voice when she spoke. "How can I not? Imagine how different Jack's life would have been if his mother had lived. Charlotte's, too. If only David had been a better father and husband…"

Lillian let her words drift off, leaving the impression there was much she didn't say. Cece held her breath, waiting, but Lillian didn't finish the thought.

For Cece this was more than mere morbid curiosity. David and Ava's marriage had been legendary in its dysfunction. Rumor had it, David—the younger and more spoiled of Lillian and Charles's two sons—had pursued and married Ava Cassettes purely for her money. Tired of playing second fiddle to his older brother, he'd wanted to start his own production company. If that was the case, Ava—the daughter of a wealthy diplomat—was the perfect mark for his ambitions. Unfortunately the marriage made them both miserable.

After Ava's death, Jack had gone to live with Lillian and

Charles. Charlotte, Jack's younger sister, had gone to live with her maternal grandparents. As far as Cece knew, neither had a particularly rosy view of marriage.

Of course, this was old news. Decades-old gossip. And since her parents were close to the Hudsons, she'd heard the story rehashed over the dinner table more than once.

When a long moment passed and Lillian didn't say anything, Cece said softly, "I've never heard you talk about Ava. It must have been hard on everyone."

"You're the product of a broken home yourself," Lillian said. "You know firsthand what it's like growing up in a war zone."

"True," she admitted. Yet, somehow her parent's rocky relationship had always felt different to her. There was an unspoken playfulness to their animosity. They'd seemed to marry and divorce one another with childish relish. Their on-again-off-again romance had been as infamous as Liz Taylor and Richard Burton's had been decades before.

Beneath the screamed accusations and the occasional hurled tumbler, there was genuine affection. Her parents had always loved each other, they'd just done so loudly and with lots of anger. It wasn't the sort of relationship she ever wanted for herself, but it suited their fiery natures.

She'd always had the sense that David and Ava's relationship was considerably less benign.

To Lillian she said, "No, my parents loved each other. And they could both dish it out as well as take it. I never felt…" She searched for the right word to describe how Jack sometimes seemed.

"Abandoned," Lillian supplied.

She frowned as she considered the word. "I never put a word to it before. But I guess Jack always had that feeling about him. As if he'd been marked by his parents' marriage. Scarred by it."

When she looked up at Lillian, it was to see tears welling in the older woman's eyes. "If only…"

Again she leaned forward to take Lillian's hand. "You certainly can't blame yourself."

Lillian's brows snapped together. "I certainly can if I choose to. David was always a difficult child. Willful and spirited. But moody as well. Charles and I coddled him too much. After Markus, the doctors told us we'd never have another child. David seemed like a miracle. But perhaps if we'd been firmer with him, he would have done a better job of living up to his responsibilities."

"Lillian, I hardly think—"

Lillian waved her hand regally. "Don't patronize me, girl, by telling me none of it's my fault. When a woman's facing death, she's earned the right to look back on her life with remorse as well as joy."

"I can hardly argue with that," Cece admitted, suitably chastised.

But Lillian wasn't done. "Believe me, it's mostly joy. But I do wish this business with Ava had worked out differently. And it frustrates me to my very bones that Jack is still paying the price for his father's mistakes. I love that boy like he was my own son and he deserves some happiness."

Cece fought the urge to chuckle. Even on her deathbed— literally—Lillian was still a spitfire. "While I doubt Jack would like to hear you say it, again, I can hardly argue with you."

"Well then, why haven't you done something about it?"

"Me?" The urge to laugh died in Cece's chest. "I'm hardly responsible for his happiness."

"Aren't you? You've been in love with him for years."

"I—"

"There's no use arguing about it. You haven't done a very good job hiding it, so you might as well do something about it. Besides, you're raising his son, and Jack could certainly use a family who loves him."

"I don't think he wants that."

"Nonsense. Of course he does."

"Even if he did want to do the white-picket-fence thing, when he finds out the truth about Theo he's going to be furious."

"So?"

"So, he'll never forgive me."

"When Charles and I first met, he thought I was a Nazi collaborator and I thought he was a spy. If we worked that out, surely you can figure out this mess you've gotten yourself into."

"You make it sound so simple."

"Why shouldn't it be?"

Cece wanted to believe that Lillian was right. But Jack was her grandson. Naturally she'd want to believe the best of him; that was the way it should be. Cece could hardly tell Lillian what her greatest fears about Jack were.

This wasn't a matter of Jack forgiving her. They'd gone way beyond that. She didn't expect forgiveness. She never had. No, this was about protecting Theo.

She knew Jack well enough to know that if he ever discovered the truth, he'd be furious with her. Angry enough to have Theo taken away from her, regardless of the fact that he didn't have any desire to be a father. Given that the Hudsons were one of the wealthiest, most powerful families in Hollywood, she didn't want to tangle with them in a court of law. True, she was not without financial resources herself. But how would a legal battle affect Theo? It simply wasn't worth the risk.

Still, she found it difficult to meet Lillian's steady gaze.

"Promise me you'll tell Jack the truth," Lillian said.

"I'll think about it." Not a lie exactly. She would think about it. She'd been *thinking* about it since she'd found out she was pregnant. Lillian didn't need to know that Cece had already decided against it, regardless of how much she might think about it.

Lillian apparently didn't sense Cece's prevarication. Seemingly at peace, she lay back against the pillows of her bed and folded her hands. "Tell him soon. Time is shorter than you think."

With that, Lillian closed her eyes. A moment later, her chest settled into the even rhythm of sleep. Cece watched her in silence, studying the face that was so dear to her. Marveling that Lillian had managed to appear elegant even in the hospital, her auburn curls perfectly styled. If her hands were a little less steady in applying her makeup, it didn't show.

Her cheekbones were still high and finely arched. Cece could hardly believe her time here was limited.

Time is shorter than you think, she'd said. And how true her words were. But wise though Lillian was about many things, Cece knew her advice about Jack was flawed. Lillian saw Jack through the eyes of a loving grandmother, Cece through the eyes of a jilted lover. But in the end it didn't matter which of them was right about Jack. This wasn't really about him, but rather about what was best for Theo.

All these years, she'd told herself she was acting in his best interest. Yes, she'd done this awful thing, but she'd done it to protect her son. And, yes, it sometimes broke her heart the way Theo longed for male companionship. But there wasn't anything she could do about that.

Jack wasn't daddy material. He'd be the first person to admit that. So what if he'd been spending all this time at Hudson Manor with Theo? It's not like he was doing it out of fondness for Theo. He was doing it because getting *Honor* made was his top priority.

She'd done the right thing.

Hadn't she?

Nine

"Tell me something, Marilyn. Why don't we have Cheryl Cassidy's phone number?"

Marilyn Davenport, one of the newer office staff at the reception desk, stammered on the other end of the line. "I wasn't aware you wanted her number, Mr. Hudson."

"Well, I do," Jack all but growled into the headset of his cell phone as he turned onto La Cienega Boulevard.

He knew he was being hard on her. He should have just called Janelle, his own assistant. But Janelle had been with him three years ago when he and Cece first dated. When he'd ended it, Janelle had made it obvious she thought he was a fool. For some reason he just didn't want Janelle to hear him all but begging for Cece's number.

Hannah—who was watching Theo today—presumably had been left at least one of the numbers where Cece could be reached, but she and Theo had taken off for the beach.

"I want her home number and her cell number," he added, just to be clear.

"Oookay." Marilyn sounded doubtful. "I can try, but I'm not sure how—"

"Call her agent first," he said as he turned his car into the hospital parking lot. "We've got his number, right? If he doesn't have it just keep calling people until you find it. Start with Martin Cassidy and Kate Thomas."

"Why?"

"They're her parents."

"Oh." She must have picked up on the frustration in his tone, because when she answered there was an edge of annoyance in her apology. "Sorry. I didn't know. I'll see what I can do. Do you want me to get you Stephen Evan's number, too?"

"Why would I want his number?"

"Well, he's the location scout. I thought maybe you wanted the numbers of everybody working on *Honor*."

"No." He yanked on the parking brake. "Just Cece's."

"Whose?"

He had to count to five before answering. "Cheryl Cassidy's."

Jack hung up on Marilyn before she could piss him off any more. It wasn't her fault. And there was no point in firing an otherwise perfectly good employee just because Cece had been avoiding him ever since she left him naked, in bed, early that morning. His mood had gone steadily downhill when he'd tried to call her and realized that she'd changed both her home number and her cell number since they'd broken up three years ago.

Since she still lived in the same house, he had to assume she'd done it solely to avoid talking to him. Damn it.

As if he didn't have enough reasons to be in a rotten mood today. He thought briefly of Cece's ridiculous comment about men processing emotion through either anger or lust. Somehow the implications of that just annoyed him more. Was he supposed to believe he didn't know what he was feeling? That his current frustration was all due to some deeper, hidden emotion he just wasn't ready to deal with? Hogwash.

Cece was jerking him around and it annoyed him. That's all there was to it. That was it.

The fact that he was so desperate to talk to Cece he was willing to torture an employee for her number only added to his irritation. This was not the way it was supposed to work.

Women he'd slept with were supposed to get less appealing, not more. Women he'd broken up with years ago were supposed to be distant memories, not haunting obsessions. Women with kids weren't supposed to even be on his radar. So what the hell had gone wrong with his plan?

As he turned the corner into the oncology ward at the hospital, Cece came into view, standing right outside of Lillian's room. For once she was dressed in something other than a ratty old T-shirt. She wore her standard jeans, but today she'd topped them with a white cotton shirt that wrapped around her waist and tied off to the side, emphasizing her glorious curves. Her hair had been piled up off her neck and appeared to be defying gravity with the assistance of a single yellow pencil.

He was struck by a memory from the months they'd spent together three years ago. He remembered waking up in the middle of the night one night to find her sitting up in bed beside him, one knee pulled up to her chest, a spiral notebook propped on the other knee as she scribbled in it. Just like today, her hair had been stabbed with a yellow pencil. The bedside light had been on, casting her in a golden glow of light. He lay there for a long time, watching her write, drifting in and out of sleep. Completely, perfectly content.

Standing in the hospital now, Jack knew what had gone wrong with his plan.

He'd never planned on Cece. He didn't want to walk away from her.

Even then he'd known their time together would be limited. Known he wouldn't get to be with her forever. That if they stayed together he'd only make her miserable.

He'd made her unhappy enough during the short time they were together. Think how much more damage he'd do in a longer relationship. He remembered how unhappy his parents had been. How his mother, Ava, had slowly faded away. Until one night she'd taken one too many sleeping pills before her customary late-night swim.

You are just like your father, she'd always said to him.

Well, maybe he was, maybe he wasn't. Either way, he'd never been willing to risk making Cece as unhappy as his mother had been. He cared for her way too much to do that.

His reaction to the sight of her now was so visceral, it took him a moment to notice she was talking to Luc and Gwen.

Gwen stood with her back resting against Luc's chest, his arms wrapped around her waist, his head close to hers. There was an easy comfort to their stance. A sort of peace in the way they casually held each other that surprised him. If he'd had to guess, he'd say neither one were given to public displays of affection. And yet they both seemed perfectly comfortable, as if they'd been holding one another all their lives.

When he approached, Luc and Gwen shifted to make room for him. Cece met his gaze, smiling with polite distance, as if she barely knew him. As if she hadn't crawled out of his bed mere hours ago.

He nodded to Luc and Gwen, ignoring Cece. If she could be cold and distant, so could he. "I thought you were heading back to Montana today."

He still couldn't believe his cousin had decided to give up life in Hollywood for a ranch in Montana, but Luc had never looked happier.

"We decided to stay in town for a few days. We're both eager to get home, but there's no rush."

Through a lucky coincidence, they'd been in town already yesterday when Lillian had been brought to the hospital.

Gwen cast a secretive smile in Luc's direction. "Besides, we have good news to share with Lillian. We figure she could use the cheering up."

"I hope the news is you've both decided to move back to L.A.," Jack said.

Cece shot him a vexed look. "Obviously the good news is that they're expecting."

Surprised, his gaze darted between Gwen and Luc. They wore identical beaming expressions. "Is she right?"

Gwen nodded, her hand dropping to her belly to cover Luc's. Only then did Jack notice that Luc's hands weren't really wrapped around Gwen's waist, as Jack had first thought, but that one rested on her hip and the other protectively cradled her belly.

"We hadn't planned on telling anyone until we were further along," Luc explained. "But with Lillian sick, we thought she'd want to know."

"Yes, of course." Cece's tone was warm, but Jack thought he saw a hint of sadness in her smile. "I'm sorry I ruined your surprise, if you hadn't meant to tell people yet."

He couldn't help wondering about her wistful expression. Was she thinking of all she'd missed out on by adopting Theo? Yes, she had a son she loved, but she hadn't experienced carrying him herself.

However, Gwen seemed not to notice Cece's regret. If possible her smile brightened even more. "It's hard to keep it a secret. We're both so excited."

Jack studied Luc's face, surprised to see just as much joy as was registered on Gwen's. Though Luc was notoriously smooth-talking, he kept his emotions close to his chest.

Given the discussion he'd had with Cece just that morning, Jack couldn't help but think how he would feel in the same situation. If Cece came to him tomorrow and told him he was going to be a father, would he be as openly happy about it? He just didn't know. Of course, in his case, it wasn't merely a question of what he wanted, but what would be best for the child.

Luc had Markus as a role model. There probably wasn't a better parent in all of L.A. Who did Jack have? His own father had been as much of a failure at fatherhood as he had at marriage.

Before he could give that grim thought much consideration, Gwen and Luc excused themselves.

"I thought you were going to go in to see Lillian?" he asked.

"Cece told us she'd just fallen asleep," Luc explained. "We're going to grab a bite to eat in the cafeteria and come back up later. Would you like to join us?"

He noticed Cece starting to edge away, shuffling her bags from one arm to another, preparing to leave. "I'll catch up with you later."

A moment later, when Cece headed for the elevator, he followed her. Without turning to even look at him, she said, "I thought you were here to see Lillian."

He ignored her comment and said, "I've been trying to reach you all morning."

"I haven't been that hard to find. I spent most of the morning at Starbucks and then I came here. It's not like I've been hiding."

"No. But you've changed both your cell number and your home number since we dated."

She shot a sideways glance at him. "As a matter of fact, I have."

He punched the call button for the elevator and asked, "Did you change your numbers because of me?"

"That's absurd, Jack. I lived in Europe for a year, of course I changed my numbers. I sublet my house while I was abroad so I'd canceled my phone service. And do you have any idea how expensive an international cell phone was three years ago? They're a little better now, but still…"

Her explanation embarrassed him. "Regardless, while you're working on *Honor,* I want your cell number. I want to know where to reach you at all times."

"Jack, this isn't necessary."

The elevator doors opened and he followed her inside, his blood pressure rising. He thought again of her comment about men and anger. Okay, maybe there was something to that. He should not be as annoyed by this conversation as he was. Now, if she would just stop pissing him off….

"I think it is," he said. Calmly. "Until you finish—"

She interrupted him. "This isn't about *Honor* and you know it. After what happened last night—"

He clasped her arm. "Regardless of what happened between us, you still have to finish the script. You've already signed the contract."

"Of course I'm going to finish it." She jerked her arm away. "With what Lillian's going through I'd be heartless not to. Regardless of the contract. What I was going to say is that Theo and I are moving out of Hudson Manor."

"You agreed—"

"When I agreed to move there, Lillian was there. It made sense. Her doctors want to keep her here for at least the next week and the nurses have already told me I can't come up here to work. So there's no point in Theo and I staying there. Besides, I've already spent hours interviewing Lillian and taking notes. It's time for me to write and I can do that best at home."

"You're just trying to avoid me."

There. He'd said it. He wanted her to stay. Not for Lillian. Not for *Honor*. But for him. For them.

But she seemed to miss his point altogether. She shot him an annoyed look. "Right. Crazy me, wanting to live in my own home. Naturally, this is all about you." The doors opened and she flounced out only to stop a moment later. When she met his gaze, the anger that had flashed in her eyes a moment ago was gone. In its place was that lingering sorrow he'd seen when she'd been talking to Gwen and Luc. "I don't know. Maybe it really is about you. I just know that being at Hudson Manor—that seeing you all the time—is bad for me. It makes me want things you'll never be able to give me."

She paused, maybe giving him the moment to protest. To set aside his fears and open up and tell her how he felt. But he didn't.

How could he, when she'd just verbalized all his worst fears? Being with him made her unhappy.

His silence snuffed out the last hint of sparkle and wit that normally lit her eyes. "And it's not good for Theo, either. Someday soon he's going to start wondering about dads and why he doesn't have one. When he does, I don't want you around confusing matters. I can't let you drift in and out of our lives whenever you feel lonely."

Great. And if it wasn't bad enough that he made her wretched, now she'd told him he was bad for Theo, too. Damn. That was the last thing he wanted.

So he kept his mouth shut about his feelings and brought up the one subject that they could agree on. "About *Honor*—"

"Well, at least you're predictable." She laughed, a sound bitter and resentful. "Here I am, pouring out my heart to you, and in the end the thing you still care about most is the family business."

When he might have stopped her again, she lashed out at

him, her tone harsher than he'd ever heard it before. "My agent will have the script to you on deadline. Until then, stay away from me and my son."

Well, she'd thrown it out there. *It makes me want things you can't give me,* she'd said.

It had been the perfect opportunity for him to step up to the plate, swing the bat and knock it out of the park. Okay, not that she really expected all of that from commitment-phobic Jack. But, jeez, it would have been nice if he'd at least gotten up off the bench. Just to let her know he was in the game.

But he hadn't. No, Jack had done what he always did. He changed the subject to one he was comfortable with. He'd pushed her away. Obviously, he wasn't any more ready for a real relationship than he had been three years ago when she'd decided to keep Theo a secret. Just when she was starting to doubt her decision, he went and justified it all over again.

Maybe she should have felt gratified. Instead, she just felt depressed. A feeling that only intensified as days passed, as she and Theo once again packed up their belongings and returned to the house. Then she realized a part of her had hoped he would change his mind. That, like Billy Crystal in *When Harry Met Sally,* he'd have some third-act internal growth and he'd rush to her house late at night just to tell her how much he loved her frown. Unfortunately, he had no such revelation.

So instead of getting her happy ending—the one she'd always sworn she didn't want—she went back to work on the story she'd been waiting her whole life to tell, even though she'd lost her enthusiasm for the project. Because if he could pretend their relationship was all about work, then so could she.

She hadn't lied to Jack when she'd told him she was done with her research and interviews. But that didn't mean her work on the script was going as planned, either. She felt...

stuck. Overwhelmed by both the drama on the page and in her own life.

So far, she was fairly satisfied with her work on the opening of the movie: A young Charles Hudson, with a sort of clean-cut, rugged wholesomeness, leaves the privilege and security of his life in Oregon—where he's been groomed to take over his family's paper mill—to join the Allied forces in Europe. Since he speaks flawless French, he's stationed in Marseilles as a spy for the Special Operations branch of the OSS.

One night, while evading Nazi troops, he ducks into a cabaret where he first sees Lillian perform. He's instantly struck by her beauty and her soulful singing. His enchantment lasts only as long as her performance. As soon as she leaves the stage she's approached by a German general notorious for his cruelty. Charles knows only a collaborator would allow a man to touch her with such possessive familiarity.

Then a few days later…

EXT. THE ALLEY BEHIND CASINO DE MARSEILLES, NIGHT

CHARLES, clutching his wounded side, stumbles into the alley. His clothes are torn and dirty. Leaning against the wall, he lifts his hand to look at the wound, revealing a large bloodstain on his shirt. He presses his hand back, trying to staunch the flow of blood. He sinks to the ground.

A moment later, the door to CASINO DE MARSEILLES opens. Light and music pour through the open door, framing the form of LILLIAN. She exits, the door closing behind her. Holding her coat tightly against the cold she walks down the alley toward CHARLES. She sees him.

LILLIAN
(crouching)
Êtes-vous les maux?

CHARLES
Yes.

LILLIAN
You are American.
German troops can be heard approaching from the street.

LILLIAN
Come with me, I will hide you.

Now passed out, CHARLES mutters incoherently.
LILLIAN wraps her arm around his waist and struggles to
stand. She reaches the top of stairs just as a German soldier
enters the alley.

And that's where Cece was stuck.

After days of fever, Charles finally wakes to find himself
in Lillian's room and...

And what?

The Lillian she knew was the matriarch of a powerful
family. She had a surfeit of wisdom, power and influence. It
was impossible to imagine Lillian as poor, insecure or afraid.
And yet she must have been all of those things.

Finding that balance was tripping Cece up. Lillian was
both seductress and heroine, both waif and sweetheart.

The audience had to go from believing she was a collaborator to sympathizing with her plight. And Cece just didn't
know if she had the skill to pull it off.

Frustrated with herself, Cece pushed her chair away from
her desk and snapped her laptop closed. For a moment, she
eyed the machine, unsure if she should open it back up and try
to get more work done or throw the dang thing out the window.

In the end, she did neither, opting instead to take a short break and check on Theo. Besides, her phone had been ringing all afternoon and she'd been ignoring it, assuming it was one Hudson or another calling to check on her progress. If she was taking a break anyway, she might as well do them the courtesy of choosing to ignore them.

Resisting the urge to pout—about her writing or about Jack—she left her office and followed the sounds of the TV through the hall to the living room.

"Hey, guys, I was—"

Maria jumped, clearly startled. The TV remote went flying out of her hand.

Cece chuckled at the expression of guilt on the nanny's face. "Maria, calm down. You and Theo are allowed to watch TV. It's no big deal."

But Maria just shook her head, the expression of horror not fading at Cece's reassurances. "Oh, Ms." She murmured it like a prayer, pointing to the TV. "You're on the show."

"What?"

"My sister called and said I should turn on the TV and there you were."

"You on TV, Mommy. You on TV." Theo bounced up and down on the sofa.

Cece retrieved the remote from the floor, just a hint of dread tingeing her confusion. Leslie Shay was being interviewed on *Access Hollywood*. This couldn't be good. Leslie was a self-proclaimed Hudson Hound. She made her living digging up dirt on celebrities and the Hudsons were her favorite mark.

Cece's stomach began to knot as she hit the rewind button on her TiVo remote. While rewinding, there flashed a picture of her with both of her parents. That had been at the Oscars three years ago, her father's third best-director nomination. One of the years he hadn't won.

The screen flashed back to Leslie. Then to a shot of Jack.

"Oh, God," Cece muttered, her heart sinking to about the level of her ankles. "Please let this be about *Honor*. Please, please, please."

As horror choked her, she pushed the play button, catching Leslie in midsentence.

"...Creative Development Vice-President of Hudson Pictures and grandson of forties starlet Lillian Hudson. Sources say that his love child is the son of screenwriter Cheryl Cassidy, daughter of Martin Cassidy and Kate Thomas." Up flashed the picture of Cece and her parents. "The couple dated three years ago. They broke up when the hunky Hudson was seen in the company of It girl Steph Papazian. Neither Ms. Cassidy nor Jack Hudson could be reached for comment."

The anchorwoman went on to speculate about the various women Jack had dated in the past three years. Cece didn't need to hear more.

She sank to the sofa, her world spinning around her. As if from far away, she heard Theo asking, "Mommy, what's a love child?"

Ten

Theo's question still seemed to hang in the air like an anvil suspended over some hapless cartoon character when someone knocked on the front door, though pounded was more like it. No need to guess who that someone was. Jack had heard. And he was here. Now.

She felt the overwhelming urge to put her head between her knees to stave off hyperventilating. She'd felt the same way the first time her agent had cut her a million-dollar deal. Panicky and anxious. Bile rising in her throat making her wonder if she could gasp for breath and puke at the same time. However, that time, it had been a good kind of panic. This was not.

Jack knocked again. Three sharp raps that somehow conveyed the full depth of his anger. Or maybe her thundering guilt just made them sound like portents of doom.

Mustering all her courage and a fair bit of defensiveness, she approached the door. Before she could answer, Jack spoke.

"Open up, Cece. I know you're in there. Your car's in the driveway." His words were as terse as his knocks had been.

She swung open the door. "Boy, that didn't take long." Her flip tone only deepened his glower. "What were you doing? Watching *Access Hollywood* in the car on your way over?"

He narrowed his gaze, but said nothing.

"Is there any chance at all you're not really mad about Theo, you're just upset about not being the first to know? Maybe worried about looking foolish on TV?"

"Cece…" He practically growled the warning.

"Okay, then. Not a time for jokes."

She knew she wasn't helping, but she couldn't seem to shut up. Her years of general smart-aleckry were catching up with her. Or maybe she'd just flipped into pure hysteria. She swallowed, trying to force out the anguished apology she knew she owed him, but before she could say anything, Jack's rapier gaze shot past her to where Theo stood framed by the doorway into the living room. His wide innocent eyes looked from her to Jack with a sort of calculated curiosity. As if he was putting the pieces together.

Boy, that sure sapped away her panic. She hoped the sight would chill out Jack, too, but she wasn't willing to risk it.

"Maria," she said. "Take Theo to his room to play, okay?"

The nanny nodded, her eyes wide with shock as she stared at Jack. Nevertheless, she shuffled Theo down the hall in no time. Leaving Cece to face Jack all on her own.

"Is it true?" Jack asked the moment Theo disappeared from view.

"How did you find out so quickly?"

"Leslie Shay was waiting for me outside of The Ivy at lunch." There was a sneer in his voice, but she didn't dare hope his anger was aimed at the poor woman. "Is it true?" he repeated.

"Do you really have to ask?"

If possible, his expression turned even stonier. "Just. Answer. The question."

"It's true. Theo is your son."

"Damn it, Cece—"

"Look, Jack, I—"

He stepped through the doorway, grabbing her roughly by the shoulders. "No. No excuses."

His grip on her arms was firm enough to bruise. His eyes seemed almost black with emotion. His anger buffeted against her, weakening her defenses—not that she tried hard to maintain them. What she'd done was unconscionable. She knew that. She deserved the full brunt of his rage.

"You had him in Europe. After we broke up. That's why you moved there."

Deserving though she may be, she couldn't let him believe she'd planned it all out.

"No, Jack. I didn't move there to hide him from you. I was already there when I found out I was pregnant."

"And that's when you decided to keep him from me?"

"No!" She struggled to free herself and was finally able to pull away. "It wasn't like that. At the time I didn't know if I was ever even going to see you again. When I moved to Europe, I wasn't certain I'd ever move back. I didn't think it mattered." She retreated to the living room, but he followed step for step. "I was hardly thinking clearly, you'd just broken my heart."

"And so you decided to get your revenge by keeping my son from me."

She spun back to face him. "Revenge? I wasn't thinking about revenge. And if I had been, I would have assumed telling you about him would be a better revenge than not telling you. You didn't want a family. You never have."

"Don't presume to tell me what I want."

"Oh, come on, Jack. I know you better than anyone. You

never wanted a family. I honestly didn't think you'd care one way or the other. Besides which, I was pregnant and living in a strange country. I made a rash decision and stuck with it."

"What about now, Cece? You and Theo spent the last two weeks in Hudson Manor." With each sentence his tone got harsher, his expression more grim. "I met Theo. I saw you both every day. You and I talked about whether or not I wanted to be a father. We slept together, for God's sake. Were you ever going to tell me he's my son?"

She met his eyes and it killed her to tell him the truth, but she knew he deserved it. "No. I wasn't."

Years of keeping people at a distance, of keeping his own emotions in check, of mastering his control—and it came down to this: He wanted to strangle Cece.

He wasn't mad. He wasn't hurt. He was furious.

He wanted to yell at her, to throw things. His muscles ached with the need to shake her, to punch the wall, to do physical violence.

If she'd been a man he would have punched her. But she was Cece. All of five foot four inches and maybe a hundred and fifteen pounds dripping wet. He couldn't punch her. Hell, he couldn't barely breath heavily without knocking her over.

Yet there she stood, chin bumped up, eyes blazing defensively, ready to give as good as she got.

He ground out the only thing he could think of to say. "You'll hear from my lawyer."

With that, he turned and stalked toward the door.

"Oh, no, no, no, you don't." Cece didn't let him leave. She propelled herself around him, blocking his exit. "I'm not about to let you make a bad situation worse by getting lawyers involved. You're mad at *me,* you talk to *me* about it."

She held her arms extended, apparently ready to physically

bar him from the door if necessary, like an elfin fairy turned defensive linebacker.

"Get out of my way."

"No, Jack. I'm not going to let you just back-burner this. We have to talk about this."

"There's nothing to talk about."

"Damn it, you know that's not true," she protested. "And what good would a lawyer do? It's not like you're going to sue me for damages. Even with my trust fund, you're worth a thousand times more than me. Hell, maybe a million times more. And you're certainly not going to sue for custody. You don't want to raise—"

"Stop telling me what I want." Just listening to her made his blood pressure spike. "You don't know what I want."

"No, Jack, *you* don't know what you want."

She said it with such smooth confidence, it only irked him more. But she was wrong, because in that instant he did know what he wanted.

He closed the last few feet between them and grabbed her by the upper arms. Instead of shaking her—which he desperately wanted to do—or kissing her—which he wanted to do even more—he moved her aside, clearing his way to the door.

"You're right about one thing, I'm not going to sue for damages or custody. The lawyer is going to draw up a prenuptial agreement. We're getting married."

"Married? Married?" Cece repeated the word twice before she realized she was talking to an empty room.

There she stood in her foyer, arms extended, shoulders raised in the quintessential "huh?" posture. She probably could have stood there repeating the word *married* for the next six hours. But Jack had already escaped out her front door and in a minute he'd drive away, leaving her with more questions than answers and more guilt than ever before.

Well, she wasn't going to just stand by and let him bully her. She dashed out the door, catching him just as he climbed into his car.

"Jack, wait," she called.

He didn't. Staring straight ahead, he jammed the key into the ignition.

"You can't just leave," she protested.

But he obviously planned to. So she opened the door and climbed into the passenger side.

"Cece, get out of the car."

"No, not until—"

"Get out of the car." He turned the key in the ignition. He looked at her, his eyes dark with anger, waiting for her to budge. When she didn't he said, "Get out of the car before I do something I regret."

"Come on, Jack, what are you going to do? Hit me?"

"I might."

He sounded deadly serious, but she scoffed. "You're not going to hit me, Jack. You're too much of a gentleman."

"You don't know what I'm capable of."

As if he were making some kind of point, he rammed the car into gear and took off.

"Well, I know I'm not afraid of your driving." He took a corner a little too fast and she had to grab hold of the handle by the door. A thunderous scowl etched his features. "Yes," she quipped. "You're very scary. Look, Jack, us getting married isn't going to solve anything."

"That's where you're wrong. It solves everything." His tone was taut with outrage. "I don't want custody of Theo. I won't take him away from you because I don't want to hurt him. But he will live with me. I want to see him every day. That's final."

"But—"

"No, Cece." He cut his gaze to her just before taking a left onto Exeter, making it obvious he was driving at random. "No arguments about this."

Fury still stewed in his eyes and she could see he meant every word he said. She nodded. "Fine, you want to see him every day, then you will. We'll find a way to make it work. We could buy the house next door and—"

"Not good enough. I want you in my house. Both of you."

"Don't be unreasonable."

Abruptly he jerked the car to the side of a road, slamming into a spot in front of an aging ranch house. He jerked the parking brake into place and killed the engine. "You don't get it, do you? After my mother died, our father just dumped Charlotte and me on my grandparents. He abandoned us because we weren't convenient anymore. I'm not going to do that to my child. If you knew me half as well as you think you do, you'd know that."

She felt his words like a solid blow to the chest. She felt the fierceness of them. The underlying sorrow. All the things he didn't say and wouldn't admit to.

"Okay," she conceded. "If you want to be a father to Theo, we'll live with you—for as long as you want. But marriage? What will that solve?"

"It will give Theo my name. He's a Hudson. It will make him a part of the family."

"You could adopt him and it would accomplish the same thing."

The look he shot her was filled with such hatred it would have caused a weaker woman to shrivel and die. "I shouldn't have to adopt my own son."

God. What could she say to that? He was right. One hundred percent. She said the only thing she could in her defense.

"I never meant for you to find out like this."

His hands seemed to spasm on the steering wheel. "Obviously. From what you said earlier, you never meant to tell me at all."

"Because I thought you were going to guess. I was so sure you'd figure it out, I never thought I'd have to tell you. Every time you were with Theo, I spent the whole time holding my breath, sure that any second you'd look into his eyes and see the truth." And now she sat here, once again holding her breath, waiting for his reply. He just stared out the windshield, saying nothing. "Come on, Jack. You had to have noticed how much he looks like you. On some level, you had to have known." Still no response. "You had to have at least guessed."

"What do you want me to say, Cece? That I'm an idiot? That I didn't see what was obvious to everyone else because I trusted you. Because I believed you were the one person in the world who would never lie to me."

The anger in his voice had morphed into bitterness. That sullen resentment was aimed not only at her, but at himself as well. And then, part of her really did shrivel and die. That part of her that had secretly still dreamed of a future with him.

She had to make this right. Whatever he asked for, she had to give him. She owed him at least that.

"Okay," she conceded. "We'll get married."

He nodded, the vein in his jaw pulsing. After a minute, he added, his voice still tight, "You were right earlier, Cece. I don't like that you've made me look like a fool. If we get married, the public will lose interest. There's nothing less exciting than a happily married couple."

She snorted. "Yeah, how are we going to pull that one off? I'm a screenwriter, not an actress."

"Then you better call your mom and get some tips." As he spoke, he pulled back up in front of her house and stopped the car. "Because I expect you to convince everyone you're madly in love with me."

As she watched him drive away a moment later, she shoved her hands deep into her jeans' pockets and frowned. Unfortunately she feared convincing everyone she loved Jack wouldn't be the problem it should be.

The truth was, she'd never stopped loving him.

"Jack my daddy?" As Theo asked the question, his tiny brow furrowed. His lips scrunched up in a grimace and his gaze shifted to one side. He sat on the side of his bed, his legs bumping against the bed rail. He couldn't look more confused if he were trying to help her with their taxes.

His expression made her heart ache. Why, oh, why, did the people she love have to suffer for her mistakes? She brushed his hair off his forehead as if she could as easily brush aside his concerns.

"Yes," she said simply. "He's your daddy."

What else could she say? Someday in the future, she'd have to explain where Jack had been during Theo's first two years and why they'd eventually gotten married. But that, thank goodness, was for another day.

"I go live Jack's house?"

"Yes." She pulled back his covers. "Do you have a book picked out?"

He scrambled off the bed to look at the bookshelf. "Free books!"

"No, it's too late for three books. Just one tonight."

"Two books!" he tried again.

"No, just one." She held out her hand and he slapped *The Runaway Bunny* onto her palm before climbing back into bed. She stretched out next to him, his head against her shoulder, each of them holding one side of the book.

Almost at the end of the book—when the baby rabbit decides to stay at home with his momma instead of running away—Theo looked up at her and asked, "Mommy, hunter shoot you?"

Confused by the odd segue, it took her a minute to figure out what he'd said. "Your friend Hunter? From swimming lessons?"

He shook his head. "From deer movie. Hunter shoot you?"

"Oh, *a* hunter. No. A hunter didn't shoot me." She studied Theo's face. "Why would you think that?"

"Bambi go live with him's daddy." Theo pointed with his finger like someone giving a lecture. "Hunter shoot Bambi's mommy."

Tears rushed into her eyes, but she blinked them away, not wanting him to see them. "Yes, when Bambi's mommy got shot, he went to live with his daddy. But that's not going to happen with us. Jack and I are getting married. You and I are moving into Jack's house together."

Theo nodded, his frown clearing.

"And apparently I need to talk to Granny Kate about what movies she shows you," Cece muttered under her breath.

A moment later, when she was pulling the sheet up to his chin and giving a kiss to Hippo Harry, like she did every night, Theo asked, "You mar-weed?"

"Yes, honey, Jack and I are getting married."

"Like in the mermaid movie?"

"Yes. Like Ariel and Prince Eric in *The Little Mermaid*."

Frankly, she thought as she kissed Theo one last time, it wasn't a bad analogy. Jack was tall, dark and handsome. Just like Prince Eric—if Prince Eric hated Ariel and had serious commitment issues.

That thought gave her pause. As she made her way to the kitchen to pour herself a much-needed glass of wine, she considered the situation.

She'd always thought of Jack as fairly commitment-phobic. After his childhood, who could blame him? Yet when push came to shove, he'd stepped up to the plate. When it came to Theo he wanted to do the right thing.

So maybe it wasn't commitment he'd been avoiding, but commitment to *her*.

Eleven

It was amazing how quickly you could throw together a wedding in a town of sycophants and wannabes. Jack decided they should marry in an elaborate wedding at Hudson Manor before the end of the month. She said he was crazy if he thought they could plan a wedding in that time, let alone have anyone show up. Turns out, she was wrong.

Of the two hundred and sixty-two people they invited, well over two hundred had sent positive RSVPs, including forty-three past Oscar winners, the heads of five other studios and a former president of the United States.

In Hollywood, all the big players respected the Hudsons enough to drop everything to attend a last-minute wedding. Everyone else was so desperate for an invitation that—rumor had it—they were being sold on eBay. If she hadn't already known the kind of money and power she was marrying into, this would have proved it.

As if she wasn't nervous enough.

To prepare for the wedding, Jack did nothing except take his Armani tux out of the closet and point his three assistants in the right direction. She, however, spent countless hours being harassed by those same assistants, sitting for fittings for the Vera Wang dress that Vera herself was personally overseeing, and making decisions she couldn't care less about.

Yes to organic orchids. No to having plumeria blossoms overnighted from Hawaii. Yes to a seven-course dinner. No to swag bags for each attendee containing Persol sunglasses, Moroccan Oil beauty products and Swarovski crystals. Yes to live music. No to having the Dave Matthews Band play the wedding march—even though he'd called her himself to offer.

All of the mind-numbing wedding plans might have been bearable if she'd felt anything other than pure dread at the prospect of marrying Jack.

Since the afternoon he'd ordered her to marry him, she hadn't seen him—not even once—not even for the rehearsal, to which he'd asked Max to attend in his stead. However, he'd visited Theo three times, each time calling ahead to verify that she wasn't there.

To hide her general feelings of fear and panic, she'd buried herself in her work, coming out to answer Janelle's demands only when absolutely necessary. It was impossible to find any joy or excitement in planning a wedding that: a) she had no say in whatsoever, and b) she knew was destined for failure.

Last she heard, Jack hated her. Since he refused to even speak with her, she couldn't imagine their marriage bringing either of them any happiness. And she was a writer; she had a great imagination.

And so it was that she found herself, on the morning of her wedding, walking down the aisle toward a man she hadn't seen in nearly two weeks and whose last words to her had been filled with bitterness and anger. Ah…her parents must be so proud.

She figured there was a decent chance that when they reached the part of the ceremony during which Jack was supposed to swear to cherish and honor her, he'd be struck dead by God. By this point, she was almost irritated enough to be cheered by the prospect.

A gazebo had been set up on the patio at the far end of the north lawn. She couldn't meet the eyes of the guests seated in chairs there. The aisle had been strewn with flower blossoms, despite her refusing them, and as she walked on them, the sweet scent rose up from the ground. A hysterical giggle bubbled in her chest as she marched down the aisle toward the twin curved steps that led up to the gazebo where Jack was waiting for her. Her father's arm was strong and steady beneath her hand. A string quartet played in the background, their music propelling her forward, past the hordes of people, past his family and her own to where Theo—the ring bearer, of course—stood clutching a white satin ring pillow in one hand and Jack's hand in the other.

Her gaze drifted up from Theo to Jack. He looked as handsome as ever, his inky hair styled into submission, his jaw rigidly clenched, his gaze hard and unwelcoming. Anyone else might mistake his expression for the seriousness such an occasion warranted. Or maybe nerves.

However, she knew him better than that. This wasn't mere tension. He dreaded this. He hated the thought of marrying anyone, let alone her. Her betrayal had cut him to the very bone and he would never forgive her. Even though she was his bride.

The ceremony passed in a blur. She tried to focus on the minister's words. Or on Theo, his expression beaming with joy. Or on the spray of orchids on the pedestal a few feet behind Jack—anything but on Jack himself.

Then the minister said the words she'd been dreading. "I now pronounce you husband and wife. You may kiss the bride."

She had no choice but to meet Jack's gaze, which wasn't as stony and distant as she'd expected, but was intense and heated. With hatred, she could only assume.

The moment stretched out. For one awful instant, she considered the possibility that he might not kiss her. That there, in front of everyone she knew and everyone she loved, he might simply turn and walk away, humiliating her and proving beyond a shadow of a doubt that not only didn't he love her but that he couldn't even force himself to touch her.

Then, with obvious reluctance, he stepped toward her and closed the distance between them. Bracing his hands on either side of her face, in a mockery of a gentle embrace, he lowered his mouth to hers.

His lips were firm and angry, bruising hers. Commanding obedience. Despite every shred of self-respect she had, she felt herself melting into his kiss, leaning into his strength. Craving his touch. Letting her body pretend—for this brief instant—that he was really hers. Letting her heart pretend his kiss was fueled by passion, not anger.

He was everything she'd ever wanted. After all the lies she'd told, after the sins she'd committed, getting him was her punishment, because, of course, she wasn't really getting him. It was all a charade. Everyone else would assume she'd gotten exactly what she wanted, but she knew the truth. Jack would never forgive her. Her lies had destroyed any chance she might have had of earning his love.

All too soon, he pulled back from the kiss. He met her gaze, his eyes an almost midnight blue. His lips straightened into a thin line.

Then he turned to face the guests, holding out his arm for her to take.

The hand she placed on his forearm trembled. She could only hope that she'd fooled everyone and that the guests assumed the tears in her eyes were tears of happiness. With her other hand, she grasped Theo's. As they walked down the aisle, he trotted along beside them, his tiny face wreathed with smiles.

I'm doing this for him, she reminded herself. *And for Jack. Because he deserves better than he's had until now.* So she'd let him have today. But when they got home things would be different. There was no way she'd let him kiss her like that in private.

Cece was the perfect bride.

With her petite curves and sable hair, she was lovely— though he sometimes thought she didn't know it. With her family and her professional background, she was almost as well connected as he was. And her wry humor and easy self-deprecation won over even the most guarded guests.

As Jack stood in a corner near the bar, a half-full glass of Patrón in his hand, he watched her work her way through the crowd. Moving from table to table, she met and charmed everyone. Among strangers, she was naturally reserved, but she hid it well.

She'd spent plenty of time at Lillian's table, making sure his grandmother was comfortable. Remarkably, news of her illness hadn't yet been leaked to the press. Cece had made a point of planning the wedding around Lillian's treatments so she could attend the wedding, both to prevent any suspicion on the part of the press and so that she could enjoy the day. It was a struggle not to appreciate her efforts. He tried.

Watching her, he itched to cross the room to her and extricate her from the crowd. To take her away to some private corner of the house, strip her clothes off and plow into her body.

It irked him that he wanted her still. Finding out about her lies and deception should have at least cooled his ardor a bit.

But he wanted her as much as he always had. Maybe he'd stayed away from her too long—or maybe not long enough. But if there was something he could have done to get her out of his system, he didn't know what it was.

The truth was, he should have married her years ago. If he had, they wouldn't have found themselves in this situation to begin with. Everything would have been much simpler. But he'd been so sure he'd be an awful husband—so certain he'd break her heart. And he wanted to save her from himself.

His instincts had proved right. They'd been married only a few minutes before he'd made her cry. For hours now, he'd been smothering the guilt over the tears he'd seen in her eyes after he'd kissed her. He'd had to remind himself that she'd caused this. She'd betrayed him. Obviously, she was more than capable of protecting herself.

"Congratulations."

Jack turned to see his cousin Devlin approaching. Dev looked as grim and forbidding as always. By way of greeting, Jack briefly raised his drink, then tossed back the last of his tequila.

Dev nodded to the bartender and ordered himself a cognac. When he had his drink, he moved back to stand beside Jack.

He didn't mind the company, though—nearly four hours into the reception, he was damn tired of making polite conversation. Even the industry talk had gotten dull. At least with Dev beside him, no one else was likely to interrupt.

After a moment, Dev—who also appeared to be watching Cece—said, "You chose well."

"Indeed." He hadn't chosen at all, which was part of the problem. He'd have been a hell of a lot more enthusiastic about this mess if it didn't feel quite so much like a prison sentence. Although if he were honest with himself, would he have picked anyone but Cece? That didn't matter, though, because he hadn't been given a choice.

Dev must have heard the sarcasm in Jack's voice, because he shot him a sardonic look. "You have doubts?"

"Not at all," he lied. "She's beautiful and charming. Everyone loves her. She's the perfect bride." If a hint of bitterness crept into his tone, he could only hope Dev wouldn't notice. "I should have married her years ago."

"I'm surprised you didn't."

Jack shot a look at Dev. "What's that supposed to mean?"

Dev shrugged. "When you were kids she was the only person you let get close to you. When I found out you were dating her a few years ago, I just assumed you'd end up married."

"Did everyone know we were together?" Jack asked.

"You didn't think you'd kept it hidden, did you?" When Jack didn't answer, Dev chuckled. "There are no secrets in Hollywood. You should know that."

Jack grunted, but said nothing—no secrets in Hollywood. Then how exactly was it that Cece had kept Theo's parentage a secret for two full years? And how was it that he'd been the last person to know the truth?

He'd wondered that often in the past few weeks. Looking at Theo now, Jack couldn't not see that Theo was a Hudson. His son.

A child—filled with love, innocence and earnestness— who would look to him for guidance. The thought made his heart stutter. It thrilled him. Terrified him.

Was that why he hadn't guessed the truth until it had been forced down his throat?

His gaze automatically sought Theo in the crowd. He found his son, curled on his Nana Kate's lap, his head resting on her shoulder, his eyes closed. Even from this distance, his exhaustion was obvious. Not surprising, though. Every time Jack had seen the boy in the past two weeks, Theo had been all but bouncing off the walls in excitement. He was thrilled to finally have a daddy.

Jack wished he could share the boy's enthusiasm. Every time he thought of himself as a father, his gut clenched with apprehension. Maybe Cece had been right to keep them apart. Maybe that was why he hadn't even let himself consider the possibility that Theo was his son. He was so damn afraid at fumbling.

Dev's gaze followed his own. "He's a good kid."

Jack nodded stiffly. "The best."

"You'll be a great—"

"Don't." Jack cut him off. "What the hell do I know about being a father? My own dad was not the best role model."

Dev shrugged. "Charles was more than a grandfather for all of us. You had him."

For the first time in weeks, the tightness in his chest loosened a bit. Maybe Dev was right. Maybe Charles was enough of a role model. He'd been a loving father and grandfather for more than forty years. And while Jack's own father had taught him almost nothing, maybe he'd be able to follow Charles's example—at least when it came to Theo. As for Cece, Jack still wasn't sure he'd be able to forgive her, though part of him wanted to.

To distract himself from his grim thoughts, he followed Dev's gaze only to realize that Dev wasn't watching Cece, as Jack had first assumed, but rather the woman to whom she was talking.

She was a petite woman, only a little taller than Cece. But unlike Cece—whose curves added to her appeal—she was rail-thin. Perhaps that's what gave her the appearance of frailty. She was lovely in a waiflike, delicate way.

It took Jack a minute to recognize her, but the proprietary gleam in Dev's eye helped Jack place her. He nodded toward her. "Valerie Shelton, right?"

Dev nodded.

"Your date?" He didn't wait for Dev to answer. Rumor had it they'd been dating. Jack knew Valerie only in passing, but he had a hard time imagining the shy young woman in a relationship with his domineering cousin. Then he remembered. "She's the heir to the Shelton media fortune, right?"

Dev nodded, a glimmer of pride in his gaze. "She's just agreed to marry me. We were waiting until after your wedding to announce it."

Surprised, he shot a look at Dev. "You're going to *marry* her?"

"It's a smart move. A connection to a media company of that size will be invaluable."

"For Hudson Pictures," Jack pointed out.

"Exactly."

Jack only shook his head. For Dev, Hudson Pictures was all that mattered. The success of his marriage was nothing compared to the success of the company.

Jack looked from Dev back to Valerie. Even an idiot could see they were poorly matched. Dev was brooding and cynical, not to mention as ruthless as a jungle predator. Val was delicate and shy—not even worthy prey—more like the flower that the predator mindlessly trampled over.

In a marriage to Dev, she'd most definitely be crushed.

Jack nearly opened his mouth to say as much. Then Cece caught his gaze and he snapped his mouth shut. He was the last person in the world who should be giving Dev advice.

After all, when it came to marriage, Jack was an idiot.

Cece was beat. After hours on her feet, surely no one could blame her for sneaking away for a short reprieve. For an hour now she'd been slowly working her way across the room, praying she could slip away from the crowd for just a few minutes. Find a coatroom or bathroom where she could kick off her shoes, fidget and rub at her eyes—all the things she'd resisted doing in public.

Finally she slipped out of the ballroom. The long narrow butler's pantry connected the formal dining room—where the post-dinner snack buffet had been set up—to the kitchen. Used to store dishes and stemware, the butler's pantry had a storage room tucked behind it. If she hadn't spent so much time as a child in Hudson Manor, she never would have known the private nooks and crannies to disappear to. The closet stored tables and chairs for large events. It wasn't a room anyone was likely to stumble upon. She'd have at least a few minutes alone.

Theo had long ago fallen asleep on her mother's lap and had eventually been carried up to sleep in the guest room where he'd stayed during their brief stint living at Hudson Manor. The reception was still in full swing. She suspected that—like all grand bashes at Hudson Manor—this party would last well into the night. She was prepared to grit her teeth through it all. But she did need a short break. Or she'd risk cracking under the strain.

Unfortunately, the moment she closed the door behind her and kicked off her shoes, she heard footsteps in the hall outside the door. She leaned against the door, eyes squeezed closed. *Walk past,* she silently prayed. *Please walk past.*

The footsteps slowed. Then stopped outside her door.

"Cece?"

Jack. Damn it.

She'd rather face all the wedding guests in her three-inch heels than face Jack. But she had absolutely nowhere to hide—no escape.

Rather than cower in the corner, she swung the door open, throwing back her shoulders and facing him head-on. "You couldn't stand to be apart from me for even a minute." She smiled tightly. "That's so sweet."

His gaze narrowed as if her comment bothered him but he didn't want to show it. "Hiding in a broom closet? That doesn't seem like you."

"It's a butler's pantry," she said glibly. "Honestly, Jack, sometimes it's like you don't know me at all."

Good thing she didn't expect him to laugh. She would have hated to be disappointed on her wedding day.

He stepped into the storage room beside her and closed the door. Though physically they had plenty of room, she still felt crowded. How like Jack to deprive her of even this moment of solitude.

"You're not planning on ducking out the back door, are you?" Jack asked.

"I might try it if I didn't think I'd be missed."

His expression tightened. For a moment, he looked just as he had during the ceremony in the moment before he'd kissed her. Suddenly the storage room felt even smaller, as if Jack and his anger took up far too much space.

"I missed you," he said.

She knew he didn't mean it the way it sounded. He'd merely noted her absence. He didn't *miss* her—didn't yearn for her. But, oh, how she wished he did. She longed for the way he used to look at her. For the tenderness with which he used to touch her. Before she'd betrayed his trust.

She tried to squeeze past him and escape from the tiny room. He put out an arm to stop her. "Let me go, Jack. I don't want to fight."

But his hand on her arm was unyielding. "Damn it, you have no idea what it feels like to want someone you're so mad at."

"You wanna bet?" She jerked her arm from his grasp and narrowed her gaze at him. "After you left me three years ago, when I went to France after you broke my heart, I sure as hell was mad then. And yes, I still wanted you. Besides, you can't imagine that I'm happy with you just now. That this is the wedding of my dreams and that I'm thrilled to be here."

He all but spit out the words. "You have no right to be mad at me."

"Of course I don't. I know I don't have any *right* to be, but I am. You all but blackmailed me into this wedding. I had no choice whatsoever."

Again he gripped her arms, but this time he hauled her against him, pressing her body against his so she felt the strength of his muscles through the many layers of their clothing, so that she felt the length of his erection hard and demanding at the juncture of her legs.

"Maybe you're right," he said. "Maybe this is my fault. But it's your fault, too."

She bucked against him, reveling in the feel of his body against hers, somehow delighting in his anger. In the roughness of his touch.

"I know," she said simply, then she arched onto her tippy toes and pressed her mouth to his. She snaked a hand around the back of his neck, molding his lips to hers.

It was stupid. Bad timing—not to mention reckless.

But she was tired of fighting with him. Tired of being his adversary. Tired of being pushed away, when all she really wanted was to feel him pressed against her, feel his heart under her hand.

She might not be the woman he loved, but for these few minutes, she wanted to feel like his bride.

Twelve

He didn't want to want her. He wanted to hate her, to hang on to his anger and indignation a little longer. But the feel of her body pressed against him and the heat of her mouth under his shattered his control—broke through his anger and wore down his defenses.

The desire he'd been burying for the past few weeks rose back to the surface. He wanted to plow into her, to bury himself in her warmth, to possess her completely. Because she was his.

His wife.

Reaching into the bodice of her dress, he cupped her breast in his hand, relishing the feel of her hardened nipple against his palm—the irrefutable evidence of her ready desire, of her need for him.

With sure and steady steps, he backed her up until her bottom bumped against the table. Frustrated by the layers of silk that kept him from her skin, he began to bunch her skirt in his hands. She moaned, rubbing herself against him.

But then she broke away from him. "We can't," she protested. "You'll wrinkle the dress. Everyone will know."

For his part, he didn't care if everyone at the reception knew what they'd done, but he certainly didn't mind obliging her.

He turned her around so she faced away from him. Pressing a hand against the arch of Cece's back, he gently eased her over. It took only a second for her to catch on. She bent forward, stretching out over the table. Kneeling, he gently folded up the back of her skirt, pulling up layer after layer until he'd revealed her legs, encased in pale silk thigh-high hose.

Running his hands up her legs, he found the garter belt that held up her hose. With a flick of his fingers, he unfastened the garters and yanked down her panties. Instantly he sought her warm center and found her dripping with moisture, ready for him.

It took him a minute to free himself from his tuxedo pants. He sent a silent prayer of thanks that he'd thought to replace the condom from his wallet they'd used when they'd had sex before. By the time he'd sheathed himself and grasped her hips, she was wiggling with frustration. He reached around her to the juncture of her legs.

He massaged the nubbin he found there, eliciting a chorus of erotic moans from her. She bucked against him. "Now," she panted.

The temptation was strong to enter her quickly, to lose himself in mindless passion. But he knew he'd regret it. He wanted to savor the moment, to sear the image of her just as she was into his mind forever: her perfect pale bottom, framed by the dangling garters of her belt and the layers and layers of ruffles of her wedding dress. And then his gaze sought her face. She looked over her shoulder at him, her eyelids half lowered, her mouth open and panting.

With one hand he continued stroking her as he sought the warm, moist center of her. Before he could plunge into her, she surged back to meet him, bringing him closer and closer to climax, impaling herself on him, using the table as leverage to push him deeper inside of her—meeting his every thrust. Cece was his match in every way—his wife.

Her climax was still rocketing through her when she heard voices in the hall outside the storage room. Behind her, she felt Jack stiffen, a sure sign he, too, had heard the voices.

She straightened, adjusting her undergarments as the skirts of her slip fell back into place. She turned to see Jack tucking his shirt back in and zipping up his pants.

To be honest, she didn't know where to begin. There was so much bad blood between them. The only time they seemed to communicate was when they were having sex.

And while I'm at it, she mentally lectured herself. *When I said I wasn't going to let him kiss me like that once we got home, I did not mean that from now on, we should just have sex in public.*

Boy they were off to a great start as a married couple. In the less than four hours they'd been married, they'd first ignored each other, then argued, then had angry—albeit earth-shattering—sex in a storage closet. Maybe she should give up screenwriting to write a personal advice column.

As she shook out her skirts, she turned to face him. "Jack, I—"

"Shh." He nodded toward the door.

The voices coming down the hall had gotten louder. She frowned, trying to place the voices. It was a woman and a man.

"I don't want to talk about this," the woman hissed. "Ever again."

"I have to see you this weekend," the man insisted.

"No." Her voice grew louder. "You can't keep doing this."

The footsteps stopped right outside the door to the butler's pantry. Both Cece and Jack leaned toward the door, straining to hear.

"I don't want to see you every time you come into town." The woman's voice sounded shrill and harassed. Like she was mere moments from hysteria. "I can't keep rehashing my one mistake."

Yet beneath the heightened emotion, Cece recognized the woman's voice. To Jack she mouthed, "Your aunt Sabrina?"

He nodded, a scowl etching into his face.

"I'm afraid Markus knows."

There was the nearly silent rasp of Sabrina sucking in a breath. "He can't know."

"He's been acting odd."

"Of course he's acting odd. His mother is dying."

"Still—" the man protested.

"No." Sabrina's voice was firm now, less nervous and more steely. "The only way he could possibly know the truth is if you told him. Did you tell him?"

"No."

"Then we have nothing more to say to each other."

There was the obvious sound of feet stomping away. First the clickety-clack of a woman's high heels, then the solid, slower thuds of the man.

A moment of stunned silence followed. Finally she muttered, "Wow, was it just me or did that totally sound like Sabrina had had an affair with that man?" When Jack didn't answer, she added, "I didn't recognize the man's voice. Who do you think that was?"

"That was my father." Jack looked at her, his expression completely devoid of emotion. "And you wonder why I thought I'd make a bad husband."

Cece made her way back to the reception separate from Jack. As she wended her way through the crowd, looking for her mother, she tried to push aside the distaste that had settled in her belly.

So apparently Sabrina and David had a past together. Sabrina had had an affair with her brother-in-law! Kinda made Cece's relationship with Jack look like the picture of health by comparison.

Dang it, she hated when people who were supposed to be responsible adults turned out to be total screwups.

Right. Unwed mother, who hid my son from his father, lied to everyone about his parentage and ended up blackmailed into marriage—like I've got room to criticize.

Exhaling a long exhausted breath, she avoided talking to anyone and ducked into the guest bathroom to check her hair and makeup. Since this part of the house had been built for entertaining on a grand scale, the bathroom was entered through a lounge area. The lounge was elegantly decorated with a settee and gilded armchair.

Unfortunately, the lounge wasn't empty. Bella stood before the mirror and sink, running her fingers through her auburn hair. Her tiny dog, Muffin, sat on the counter beside her evening bag. Muffin had a frilly lavender scarf tied around her neck, which matched Bella's bridesmaid's dress. Bella smiled when she saw Cece.

"Hey," Cece said by way of greeting.

"Hey, yourself."

Before Bella could look at her too closely, Cece threw out something to distract her. "You're positively beaming. Did you just win the lottery or something?"

"Even better." If possible, Bella's smile grew even brighter. "I just got Uncle David to cast me as Lillian in the movie."

"Wow, that's fantastic!"

Bella threw her arms around Cece in an impulsive hug. "I know! I'm so excited I can't stand it."

"Wait, your uncle David?" Jack's father. Walking down the aisle, she'd barely seen him in the sea of faces. Though obviously—after the incident in the butler's pantry—she knew he was here. But... "I didn't know he was directing the movie."

"Well, sure. He doesn't normally work with Hudson Pictures, but he was adamant about wanting to do the project."

Cece frowned. "But don't they have to do auditions, all that stuff?"

"Boy, you really have had your head buried in the wedding plans."

"That and working on the script."

"Uncle David's been having people read for the part for weeks now." Cece knew they were doing preliminary casting. Because of the time crunch, they were working on just the initial treatment she'd written and a few early scenes. Bella waved a hand, her expression turning a tad bitter. "He should have cast me first thing, but no, they had to talk to 'big talent' first." Bella made air quotes with her fingers, her annoyance obvious.

It was hard not to chuckle at Bella's indignation. Cece made the effort, since she suspected Bella wouldn't appreciate the humor. "I take it you thought he should just cast you without an audition?"

Bella stiffened. "Of course not. But you wouldn't believe how hard I had to fight just to get a reading. No one in this family takes me seriously. They seem to think I'm just playing at being an actress." She pointed a finger at Cece, her expression fierce. "But just wait until we start shooting. I'm going to act the hell out of this part."

Cece laughed. "They won't know what hit them."

"Exactly." Bella's expression turned shrewd. "I don't suppose I can get an early look at the script."

"I'll see what I can do."

"Thanks." Bella turned back to the mirror and ran her hands down her hips, smoothing the lines of her bridesmaid's dress. When she turned to leave, she asked, "So how's it feel to finally be Mrs. Jack Hudson?"

"Great." Cece tried to infuse the word with more enthusiasm than sarcasm. After a second, she squinted at Bella. "Wait a minute. What do you mean, *finally?*"

Bella shrugged, her delicate shoulders perfectly mimicking Lillian's signature Gallic shrug. "Well, you've been in love with him for years, right?"

"Is there anyone who doesn't think I'm in love with him?"

"Is it supposed to be a secret?"

Cece spoke through gritted teeth. "I guess not. How reassuring to know that everyone knows exactly how pathetic I am."

Bella smiled wryly. "It's not pathetic to love your husband. It's charming."

With that, Bella drifted out the door, enveloped in her own little cloud of joy, unaware of how concisely she'd summed up Cece's current dilemma.

"No," Cece muttered to herself. "It's only charming if your husband loves you back. When he's completely disdainful of you, it's just pathetic."

Since contemplating her own love life was just too depressing an endeavor on her wedding day, she focused her attention on the conversation she and Jack had overheard.

It was no surprise she hadn't recognized David's voice. She'd been only six when Jack's mother, Ava, had died. After her death, David had spent most of his time abroad, only rarely coming home to Hudson Manor. So she'd met him only a handful of times.

But apparently, on those rare occasions he made it back to the States, he took the time to harass poor Sabrina. Of course, if she had had an affair, she wasn't entirely blameless. But she loved her husband. Any fool could see that.

Just as any fool could see that Jack and David were nothing alike. So why couldn't Jack see it?

She and Jack did not make love on their wedding night.

Despite the luxury of the four-thousand-dollar-a-night penthouse suite he'd rented at Chateau Marmont for them to stay in the night of the wedding, he didn't come near her.

She wanted to feel as indifferent about his rejection as he so obviously felt about her. But, if her conversation with Bella was any indication, she'd be fooling only herself. Apparently everyone in the family—maybe everyone in Hollywood—knew she loved Jack. Honestly, she didn't know what she wanted more: for them to be wrong or for Jack to return her feelings.

But from the moment they stepped through the door of the elegant suite and Jack began ignoring her, it was evident that neither was likely to happen anytime soon.

Since arriving at the hotel at nearly midnight, he'd showered, booted up his laptop to check his e-mail and then called Tokyo to talk to an investor, on his wedding night—on *her* wedding night.

She might have forgiven his behavior in the storage room. She couldn't forgive this.

By one o'clock, she'd showered. She'd considered, dismissed and reconsidered every item of clothes in her suitcase, from the corset and garter belt she'd worn under her wedding dress to the gossamer chiffon silk peignoir to the yoga pants and tank top she usually slept in. When she peeked out of the bedroom to see him on the phone, she picked the yoga pants and tank top. Shoving the peignoir into the depths of the suitcase, she cursed her stupidity for buying the damn thing. What had she really expected? That while standing at the altar, marrying a woman who'd betrayed him, he'd suddenly realize he loved her and on their wedding night, he'd sweep her up into his arms and make tender love to her?

Then she paused in the act of zipping the bag and sank to the side of the bed. No. She hadn't expected that. But some part of her had hoped for it. With a groan she buried her face in her hands. Oh, she could hide away that peignoir, but suppressing the yearnings of her heart wasn't as easy.

Finally, she stood, resolve stiffening her spine. She wanted a real marriage to Jack and she was going to fight for it.

Marching into the sitting room, she snatched his iPhone out of his hand and clicked it off.

Jack narrowed his eyes at her. "You just hung up on—"

"I don't care who I just hung up on. You're lucky I didn't throw the damn thing out the window."

"The windows don't open."

"Like I said—you were lucky."

Jack stood, propping his hands on his hips. "You're acting like a child."

"You're acting like an ass." She tossed the phone on the sofa, all but daring him to go for it. Mimicking his posture, she propped her hands on her own hips. "Is this the way it's going to be?"

"Is this the way what is going to be?"

"Our marriage. Is this really the way you want it to be? Long stretches of treating each other like strangers, punctuated by impulsive sex in public places? Where we don't have to take responsibility for our actions or—God forbid—have a conversation afterward?"

"Is that what this afternoon was?"

"Wasn't it?" Suddenly her anger and irritation drained away. "This isn't the kind of marriage I want to have with you."

His expression darkened. "Then you should have—"

"Yeah, I know. I should have told you when I discovered I was pregnant. But I didn't." She tilted her head to the side. "I know that what I did was awful. I just don't know how to apologize for it."

"You can't."

"Exactly. I can't apologize. I'm not even going to try. But would you please just listen to me try to explain?"

He didn't answer. His expression didn't even flicker.

Well, hey, he wasn't throwing her out. And at least he hadn't lunged for the phone and placed a call to Bali. So maybe there was hope yet.

Now if only she could think of what to say. Here she was, a professional writer—an award-winning writer—and for the life of her, she couldn't think of how to phrase the explanation she'd pleaded with him to listen to.

"Back before I had Theo—before you and I even dated— I used to take my laptop and go work at this little café on State Street called Café Rica. It wasn't fancy—not the kind of place people go to be seen. You wouldn't be caught dead there."

She flashed him a game smile. When he didn't return it, she continued undaunted. "It's the kind of place stay-at-home moms take their kids for a snack or for lunch. They make the best chocolate cake doughnuts you've ever tried."

His eyes narrowed, and she could tell she was losing his attention.

"The thing is, before Theo, I would go there with my laptop and see these moms with their kids. They never got to enjoy their meals. They had kids climbing all over them." She gestured as she spoke, miming the kids climbing over her. "It was all just sippy cups and baby wipes and peanut butter and jelly sandwiches. I'd see these moms and think that their lives just seemed *so small*."

She looked up at Jack. His expression had cleared. For the first time in weeks he seemed to be listening to her.

"Now, whenever Theo and I need a treat, we go back there. Every once in while, there'll be some young woman with a laptop, working away. She'll look over and I'll see it in her expression. That…" She had to search for the right word. "…disdain."

Jack nodded. "And you regret the choices you made."

A smile teased at her lips. "No. Not at all. I look at those women, and, compared to my life, *their* lives seem so small. So empty.

"That's the thing about becoming a parent. It's this huge deal. But you have no idea how huge until you're already there."

She was watching Jack's expression as she spoke and the pain that flickered across his face made every cell of her body ache. He understood what she hadn't until too late. He knew what it meant to be a father.

"When I made the decision not to tell you I was pregnant, I didn't know what it meant to be a parent. I didn't understand what I was depriving you of. And once I did, the damage was already done."

She shrugged. "It's as simple as this. I made a mistake. One that I didn't know how to undo. And you probably can't forgive me. If you want to be mad at me for the next fifty years, I'm okay with that. What I'm not okay with is you treating me like crap to try to get back at me. That's not the kind of family I want our son to grow up in. This is a marriage, Jack. It's not revenge."

* * *

It was on the tip of his tongue to deny it. But how could he?

Everything he'd done for the past two weeks had been fueled by blind anger. Right up until the moment he'd climaxed inside of her in the butler's pantry of Hudson Manor.

And that was the moment he'd realized the truth: He didn't hate Cece, he loved her.

He loved her unstylish curves and that funny little bump on her nose. He loved her snarky sense of humor. And her unpretentious, pedestrian love of action movies. He loved the way she'd raised their son. Hell, he'd probably loved her since they were teenagers. He—

Mentally, he cut himself off. Damn it, he was starting to sound like one of those sappy characters from a Nora Ephron romantic comedy. Next thing he knew he'd be waxing poetic about how she ordered her sandwich or the way she smelled like cinnamon Altoids. The way she… Damn it, he was doing it already.

Knowing he loved her, how could he continue treating her the way he had? How could he continue to push her away? Until now, his anger had given him the strength to hold her at arm's length. But he couldn't do it forever. Eventually she'd wear him down. She'd wiggled past his defenses. Their marriage would become a real marriage. And from there it would all be downhill.

He didn't want to hurt her. Yes, he was behaving badly. Not out of anger, but to protect her. After all, what the hell did he know about being a father or a husband? Everything he'd done so far in their relationship had made her miserable. She'd said it herself.

Despite everything she'd done, it still came down to this: he would break her heart. In the end, he would destroy her, just as his father had destroyed his mother. As he was trying to destroy Sabrina now. And the longer Jack and Cece were together, the worse the damage would be.

Yet there she was, staring up at him—her eyes wide and expectant—waiting for his response.

So he said the only thing he could think of to say. "You're right. This isn't the kind of marriage either of us want." Picking his phone up off the sofa, he headed for the door. "Wait a month and then file for divorce."

Thirteen

Cece did her best to ignore her impending divorce. She hadn't mentioned it to Jack. Hadn't talked about it with Theo—goodness knows he was confused enough as it was. Hadn't even let herself think about it.

To be honest, she hadn't really decided if she was going to let Jack go through with it. As disgruntled as the idea of a loveless marriage made her, Jack's new idea—a very short loveless marriage followed by a quick and dirty divorce—seemed much worse. Unfortunately she had no idea about how to talk him out of it.

A week after the wedding they appeared together in public for the first time at the premiere of *At Second Glance*, a thriller Jack had done a lot of work on. Despite the fact that most of the Hudson Pictures premieres were held at Grauman's Chinese Theatre, this premiere was held at the Westwood Crest, the same theater she and Jack had gone to the night they'd first made love. She hoped rather than believed that he'd influenced the location of the premiere and that he'd done so as a sign he was beginning to forgive her.

Wearing yet another Vera Wang dress—this one a lovely glittery silver—Cece couldn't help thinking bitterly that if Jack was going to push for a quick divorce, at least she was getting some really great clothes out of the marriage.

Other than the premiere, she'd buried herself in her work, spending as many as twelve hours a day at her computer, barely sleeping, wandering around the house muttering lines of dialogue until they sounded right.

Maria thought Cece had gone crazy. Theo pretty much ignored her behavior. She'd worked on four other scripts in his short life and he was familiar with her many quirks. Besides, he was too busy exploring Jack's home to pay her much attention.

For her part, she'd allowed the movers to unpack all of her belongings at Jack's Malibu contemporary prairie-style house. True, they might just have to repack them in a month, but for now, Cece was pretending she was here to stay. And, she had to admit, as much as she'd always loved her little Santa Barbara cottage, she was totally digging Jack's panoramic views of both the canyons and the ocean.

But the truth was, she was just too stubborn. Keeping her things in boxes seemed like too great a concession. And she wasn't going to let Jack boot her out of his life without a fight.

But first, she had to finish this script. And to be honest, she didn't mind. Burying herself in the universe of World War II espionage was preferable to dealing with her own life.

Which was why Cece found herself back at Hudson Manor a mere week after her wedding. She'd loaded Theo into the car and headed over just after lunch.

When he'd spent so much time at Hudson Manor during

the planning of the wedding, Theo had taken to calling Lillian Granny Lilly, which she seemed to love. Following an afternoon for reading books and doing puzzles with Granny Lilly, Theo had fallen asleep curled up on the sofa with his head in her lap.

"I'm surprised to see you so soon after the wedding, my dear." Lillian stroked Theo's hair as she spoke.

"Hey, you're the one who set the deadline for making *Honor*," Cece quipped. Then she blanched, as she realized how her words sounded. "I meant the deadline for the sixtieth. Not the other…um…"

She couldn't quite bring herself to use the word *deadline* again as embarrassment burned in her cheeks. Apparently having her heart broken had turned her into an insensitive idiot.

Lillian merely chuckled. "Goodness, girl, there's nothing wrong with speaking frankly. And you're right. My cancer is setting the timetable. I should just be thankful you're willing to work on your honeymoon."

Cece smiled tightly. "I just managed to pull myself away."

Lillian frowned. "Is there trouble in paradise?"

"Trouble? No." Lillian didn't need to know that her grandson was acting like a jerk. "I just stopped by to see if you'd had a chance to look at the script."

Two days ago, she'd finished a passable draft of *Honor.* She'd immediately printed it and had it couriered over to Lillian for her to read. No one else—not even Jack—knew she was so far along in the script. Lillian's opinion was the one that mattered most. It had been a struggle to wait even this long before coming over to badger Lillian for her thoughts, which was why Lillian's frowning hesitancy unsettled Cece. "It certainly had enough action in it."

Cece looked from Lillian to the sheaf of papers sitting on the table beside Lillian's chair. "You didn't like it, did you?"

"Plenty of snappy dialogue." The words might be complimentary, but Lillian's tone said it all.

"Oh, my God. You hated it."

Then Lillian added, as if to placate Cece, "And it was very factual."

"Factual?" Devastated, Cece sank to the edge of the sofa. "I wrote my heart out. And the best you can come up with is *factual?*"

"It reads very much like a Cece Cassidy script." There was a note of dissatisfaction in Lillian's voice.

Stung, Cece snapped, "You do know you hired Cece Cassidy, right?"

Lillian stiffened and looked down the bridge of her nose at Cece. "My dear, you have always had a very smart mouth."

Suitably chastised, Cece murmured an apology.

Lillian didn't acknowledge it. "That is what I mean when I said it read like a Cece Cassidy script. You have a smart mouth, but not a smart heart."

"What is that supposed to mean?"

"My dear, it means that you went too easy on us. You pulled your punches."

"I did?"

"Indeed. You wrote as though our marriage was a foregone conclusion."

"I see." But she didn't. She felt as confused as ever.

Lillian must have sensed Cece's confusion, because she said, "You knew we were going to end up together, so you treated us as if there were no doubts—no obstacles. You wouldn't write one of your disaster movies in which the hero was never at risk, now, would you?"

"Well, no," Cece admitted, a little chagrined. Fear for the main character's safety was precisely what kept audiences on the edge of their seat.

"In a romantic movie, the audience must believe the couple might not get together. That there are obstacles in their way."

"Yes, I know that." Cece felt her cheeks warming. It was no fun being lectured about how to do your job. "But this is a biopic. And in real life—"

"It is especially true in real life. Surely you don't believe the Nazis were the only thing keeping us apart."

"I—" She wanted to protest, but realized she couldn't. Suddenly she understood what Lillian meant when she said Cece had been pulling her punches. It wasn't just that she'd been going easy on the characters. She'd been holding back. Her own fears had gotten in the way of letting her characters be truly vulnerable. "You and Charles always seemed to just fit. I guess I thought it had always been that way."

"Of course it wasn't. No matter who you are, no matter when you live, there are always reasons not to love, not to trust, to be afraid of falling in love."

"What was your reason?"

She needed to know. Not just for the script, but for her own life as well. Because if Lillian and Charles made it work, then maybe there was hope for her and Jack, too.

"My reasons aren't important. To make the script work, you must find your own reasons. You must look in the story and find the truth that speaks to you. If you had been me, why would you be afraid to fall in love? Just remember, there are a hundred—a thousand—reasons not to let yourself fall in love. And only one reason to let yourself love."

"And what's that?"

"Because without the other person, you'll never be whole."

If he had only a month of living with his son, Jack had every intention of making the most of that time. With the exception of the preproduction work he was doing on *Honor,* work could wait. Hudson Pictures would still be there after his divorce. At the same time, he didn't want to spend time with Cece. He also didn't want her to know exactly how much time he was spending with Theo.

When it came time for her to file for divorce, he didn't want her to have qualms separating them.

So in the week since their wedding, he'd mastered the art of avoiding Cece, which was no easy task when she worked from home. However, she'd spent the last two days sequestered in the guest bedroom she'd commandeered as an office putting the finishing touches on the script. Lillian, he'd figured out, had seen a version of the script a few days before. He could only assume her feedback had been helpful, because Cece had been hard at work ever since returning from Hudson Manor.

With Cece so busy, talking Maria into bringing Theo by the studio was easy enough. Jack just hadn't expected his own father to be there.

However, even if he wanted to avoid his father indefinitely, he couldn't. As soon as Jack, Theo and Maria exited his office for an impromptu tour of the lot, they ran into David.

His gut clenched at the sight of his father. They'd barely spoken at the wedding. And to be honest, he still couldn't shake the distaste he felt after hearing his father and Sabrina talking.

David nodded to Jack. "Congratulations."

"Thanks." Jack waited for his father to look at Theo, who stood beside him fidgeting. When he didn't, Jack gently nudged the boy toward Maria and said to the nanny, "I heard it's Janelle's birthday and someone brought in cupcakes from Sprinkles for her. Her office is just down the hall." He nodded in that direction. "Why don't you and Theo go grab one before they all disappear? I'll catch up with you."

Maria, still looking a little starstruck, nodded and moved to shuffle the boy off for a snack.

However, Theo slipped his hand into Jack's and looked up at him with large blue eyes. "You go, too, my daddy?"

Something tightened around his heart as Jack knelt down to Theo's eye level. "I'll be there in a minute."

Theo shot a suspicious sidelong glance down the hall, seeming to weigh the relative safety of eating cupcakes in a strange place. Finally, he nodded his head, his expression serious. "Soon," he ordered.

"Yes," Jack agreed. "Soon."

When they were out of earshot, he turned to his father. "Why do I think you didn't stop by my office just to see Theo again?"

David shot him a baffled look as he prowled into Jack's office. "Why would I do that?"

"You know he's your grandson, right?"

David shrugged. "I think most of America knows it."

Jack shook his head, following him into the office. "You don't ever change, do you?"

Jack's office was decorated in the sleek midcentury modern furniture he preferred, and David slouched into one of the sling back leather chairs before answering.

"What?" Even at fifty, David managed to instill the question with an adolescent insolence.

"That's your grandson," Jack pointed out as he wedged his hip against the corner of his Heywood-Wakefield desk. "And you're not the least bit interested in him, are you?"

"He's what? Four years old? Why would I be?"

Jack gritted his teeth. "He's two."

"Whatever." David leaned forward in his chair. "Did you know Markus is talking to cinematographers about *Honor?*"

"Sure. It came up. I guess you think—"

"That I should get to hire my own crew? Yes, I do. That's the way it's done."

"True, but this is the most important movie we've ever made. He wants the best."

"And he thinks I don't want the best in the industry?" David scowled. "He knows how important this is to me. I told him at the wedding."

Something clicked in Jack's mind. "That's why you came to the wedding, isn't it? You came solely so you could harass Markus about *Honor.*"

"Of course not." But the hesitation before his answer said it all. Jack had guessed right.

Jack pushed himself away from the desk. "You wouldn't have come to my wedding if it hadn't served your own needs. You're not even interested in meeting your grandson. Just out of curiosity, were you any more interested in Charlotte and me when we were children?"

A disgruntled scowl settled over David's face. "What's the point of rehashing past mistakes?"

"What's the point?" Jack repeated incredulously. "The point is, you made me into the man I am today."

"Well, then you're welcome."

"I didn't thank you. I'm not exactly proud of the man you made. I've been self-centered and untrusting. I've been unhappy."

His father chuckled bitterly. "Yeah. Who isn't?"

"A lot of people aren't." Cece was the first to come to mind. And for some reason, he thought of his own mother, who had always been so unhappy. "Do you remember what you told me just before Mom died?"

David looked exasperated but didn't reply. "Why would I?"

"The two of you had just had another big fight. She was crying, you were storming out and I asked you why you couldn't be nicer to her. I asked why you didn't love each other anymore. Do you remember what you said?"

"Obviously you do," David said.

"You said, 'Loving a woman is easy. Making her happy is impossible.'"

David snorted with smug laughter. "That sounds like me."

"Then you said, 'Someday you'll know what I mean.'" Jack shook his head ruefully. "The stupid thing is, I believed you."

Less than a week later, his mom had been found dead in the swimming pool. There'd been plenty of rumors that, at nine, he surely hadn't been meant to hear. Rumors that it was suicide. Of course, no one knew for sure, but what emotionally stable woman would take that many sleeping pills before swimming?

Standing at his mother's graveside, he'd sworn to himself that he'd never make anyone as miserable as his father had made his mother. And in trying not to follow in his father's footsteps, he had done to Cece exactly what he'd sworn he would never do.

Now, as he excused himself, he realized how faulty his logic had been. Just because his father had dysfunctional relationships, that didn't mean he would. Walking across the lot, Jack could only shake his head. Like he'd needed the reminder that David was an asshole.

Then he stopped in his tracks. In fact, he *had* needed the reminder.

His father's treatment of Theo had been classic David Hudson: self-absorbed, arrogant, dismissive.

It was the way he'd treated Jack and Charlotte throughout their childhood. It was dispassionate and uninvolved at best.

To be honest, it was a vast improvement over the way David had treated Ava. To her he'd been openly critical, sometimes outright cruel. And Ava, for her part, had taken it. She never fought back. Never defended herself.

Invigorated, Jack walked down the hall. Following the

sounds of giggling, he opened the door to Janelle's office. An A-list actress with two kids of her own stood beside them. She'd pried the two-tone dot decorations off the tops of two cupcakes and stuck them to her eyelids to make fake eyes. Theo laughed out loud, bouncing slightly on the chair in a *more, more, more* kind of way.

Jack felt his heart expand just watching him. Suddenly, he understood what Cece had been talking about: the greatest gift he'd ever been given.

He couldn't imagine treating a child—let alone his own son—with the dismissive negligence that David had treated Theo. He knew in that moment that Theo would always be precious to him. He would always love his son. He would always be devoted to Theo in a way his father had never been to him.

So if he wouldn't treat Theo the way his father had treated him, then why had Jack assumed he would treat Cece the way his father had treated his mother? For that matter, why had he assumed Cece would let him get away with that kind of behavior? Cece wasn't as emotionally frail as his mother had been. Cece was a fighter.

She'd always given as good as she got. He didn't have to coddle or protect her—certainly not from himself.

He wasn't his father.

It came down to that one simple fact. He didn't have to make the same mistakes his father had made. He certainly hoped Theo would never make the mistakes he'd made.

Jack's father might be a total bastard. But that didn't mean he had to be.

When he stepped into Janelle's office, she looked up with a smile. Maneuvering around the cupcake antics, she picked up a stack of papers from the printer as she crossed the room.

"Cece e-mailed in a draft of *Honor.* I was just coming to bring it to you. I know you wanted to see it right away."

He accepted the pages from Janelle with a nod. "I'll take a look at it right after lunch with Theo."

Thumbing through the pages, he stifled a feeling of foreboding. The script would be excellent. He knew it would be. Yet its completion marked the end of his excuses to talk to Cece, which left nothing for them to discuss except their relationship. His work on *Honor* might be coming to a close, but his work on his marriage was just beginning.

It was an odd thing, to work eighteen-hour days on a script, to have it completely consume your life, and then to be abruptly done with it. Just before lunch, she'd e-mailed the script for *Honor* to Janelle, Jack's assistant. Only after hitting Send did she emerge from the office to realize the house was completely empty. Jack, Maria and Theo had apparently all left for the Hudson lot and she hadn't even noticed until she found the note stuck to the refrigerator.

So she did all the things she always did after finishing a script. She showered, she ate a decent meal, she hit the supermarket to replenish their depleted stores. She had the bizarre experience of seeing her own wedding picture emblazoned on the tabloids. The woman in the checkout line behind her had given her several pointed looks.

Even without that, the experience of shopping alone was odd. It had been years since she'd been to the grocery store alone. Not only did she miss Theo, but she missed Jack as well.

Three hours later, when she heard the sound of the key turning in the front lock, her heart leaped in her chest. From her spot in the kitchen, she could see Jack's tall form through the textured glass of the front door. Quickly wiping her hands clean on a dish towel, she dashed forward to open the door for Jack. In his arms, he cradled a sleeping Theo. In one hand, Theo clutched his beloved Hippo Harry. Atop his head perched an oversize gimme cap advertising one of Hudson Pictures' big summer movies.

She tiptoed alongside Jack as he carried the sleeping boy to his room and deposited him on his bed. A moment later, she eased the bedroom door closed and found herself alone with Jack. Only then did she realize that it was the first time they'd been alone since their ill-fated wedding night. Suddenly the absolute conviction she'd felt while rewriting *Honor* wavered under the force of her nerves. Besides, there was something quiet and contemplative about Jack's mood that she found troubling.

Creeping down the hall back toward the kitchen, she shoved her hands into her back pockets. "I guess he had a good time at the studio."

Jack nodded. "You're not going to give me a hard time about bringing him there, are you?"

She shot him a surprised look. "Should I?"

"A couple of weeks ago, you seemed pretty concerned about his being corrupted by life in Hollywood."

The memory made her chuckle. "Yeah, I guess that was a little crazy, huh?"

He raised an eyebrow but said nothing. Jack Hudson was no dummy.

Just shy of the kitchen, she turned to face him. "He's a Hudson. Moviemaking is in his blood. Just like it's in mine. I think I was just scared of your finding out the truth about him."

"And now?" As Jack asked the question, he moved closer to her, cornering her against the wall. There was something predatory about his gaze that made her pulse leap.

Before she could answer, the oven timer went off. She nearly jumped out of her skin, before ducking off to grab some oven mitts.

Jack just looked at her like she was crazy. "What's that?"

She swung open the oven door and eyed the pie inside. Crispy crust, bubbling filling. Looked perfect. Gingerly she removed the product of her afternoon's work. "A cherry pie." Setting it on the countertop to cool, she explained, "I always bake after finishing a script. It helps quiet me down."

Of course, this time around, it wasn't only her script-related nerves she was trying to quiet. But Jack didn't yet know there was more at stake than just a movie.

He looked at the pie. "Cherry pie, huh? That's my favorite."

"I know." She sucked in a deep breath and prepared to jump into unfamiliar waters: emotional honesty. "I remembered from when we were together. To be honest, Jack, one of the reasons I baked it was to butter you up."

"I see." He'd followed her into the kitchen and now rested his hip against the counter. He was still dressed for work and somehow the Armani suit he wore still looked crisp and fresh. It made him look all the more imposing. "So you're filing for divorce then."

His expression had grown coolly distant, which made what she was about to say that much harder. "No. Just the opposite, in fact. I'm not going to divorce you, Jack."

For perhaps the first time since she'd met him, he seemed at a loss for words. His brows snapped together and he muttered an inelegant, "Huh?"

"After a great deal of thought, I've decided that you're stuck with me." She plucked the oven mitts off her hands and tossed them aside. "You may not want to admit it yet, but you love me. And I love you, which has probably been obvious for a while now. At least, that's what everyone keeps telling me."

She waited for him to deny it, but he only smiled. A slow cocky smile that turned her insides to goop and made her wish she had some sexy little outfit on that would level the playing field a bit.

But since she wasn't and since her powers of verbal persuasion had always been stronger than her powers of seduction anyway, she kept talking. "When I was talking to Lillian, she said something interesting. She told me there were lots of reasons for her and Charles not to be together, and only one reason for them to risk falling in love and that was because they would never be happy without the other."

Because she was afraid he wasn't taking her seriously enough, she closed the distance between them and got right in his face.

"Well, I figure we've got two reasons. We have Theo and that happiness thing."

His lips twitched with laughter. "So you're saying you'll never be happy without me?"

Irked by his smugness, she lied with a smirk, "No, I'm saying you'll never be happy without *me*. I'd be fine."

His hand snaked out and grabbed her. He pulled her to him for a quick, possessive kiss, one hand on the back of her head, the other anchoring her hips against his. "Too bad. You're stuck with me now."

She pulled back and stared at him, a little suspicious. "Am I?"

"Absolutely." For a moment his humor faded and his expression turned serious. "I never should have told you to file for divorce. The only reason I did it was because I was afraid I was going to make you miserable. And in trying to protect you from that, I ended up making you miserable anyway."

There was a hint of anguish in his voice. As if he were still afraid of the power he held over her. In truth, it scared her a little, too. They had both hurt each other in the past. And there were no guarantees that they wouldn't make mistakes in the future, too. But if they did, they'd figure it out.

Because she knew what he was thinking of, to him she said,

"I'm not your mother. I'm not going to let you make me miserable. Maybe I won't always be as deliriously happy as I am right now, but if I'm not, we'll work on it together."

He quirked an eyebrow. "Deliriously happy?"

She punched him playfully on the arm. "Yes. I figure you're about two seconds away from telling me that you love me. That you can't imagine living without me. That—"

He kissed her again. When he pulled away he said, "I love you. I can't imagine living without you. You've made me deliriously happy. That good enough?"

She cocked her head to the side and pretended to consider. "It'll do. But it wouldn't hurt if you added that you'd read the script and it knocked your socks off."

"There's plenty of time for that later."

"Later?"

"Sure. Later." Then he swept her up in his arms and headed for the bedroom. "Right now, I want to make love to my wife. Give her that wedding night she deserves."

Epilogue

"I see what you mean." Jack took a sip of his coffee to wash down the bite of doughnut. "That really is the best chocolate cake doughnut I've ever had."

Sitting across the table from him, Cece smiled. They sat on the outdoor patio of Café Rica, the little restaurant she'd told him about. Theo sat happily on his knees on the chair between them, his own chocolate doughnut cut into bite-size pieces carefully balanced on the rim of his plate of scrambled eggs.

"More doughnut, my daddy," he said gleefully.

"After you finish what you have," Cece chided gently. She took a bite of her own doughnut, then briefly closed her eyes in ecstasy. When she opened them again, she asked, "Did you ever get in touch with Charlotte?"

"I did. I finally tracked her down in New Orleans. She apologized for not making it to the wedding."

"She travels so much with your grandfather, I didn't really

expect her. What about Montcalm? Did she think she'd be able to talk to the owner about filming *Honor* there?"

"Apparently she knows the guy. She said she thinks she can talk him into it, but that it'll really cost her."

Cece raised her eyebrows speculatively. "Hmm. That's interesting. Did she say why?"

"Nope. I got the feeling the owner of Montcalm isn't someone she likes very much."

"Charlotte's always been the picture of sophisticated grace." Cece grinned impishly. "I'd like to meet the man who can ruffle her feathers."

Theo looked up from his plate, tilted his head to the side and asked, "Aunt Charlotte have feathers?"

Jack met Cece's gaze across the table and they both chuckled.

Cece held out the boxed milk for him to take a sip. "No. She doesn't have feathers."

Watching his wife and son, Jack felt his chest tighten with emotion. For once, instead of pushing it all aside, he let it in. Just enjoyed it.

Later, after they'd finished their breakfast and packed up Theo's crayons and sippy cup, Jack stood, lifting Theo onto his shoulders. They were all heading over to the lot for the day. Bella had her first costume fitting this morning. Theo was eager to see Miss Bella—as he called her—all dressed up like Granny Lilly. Jack was looking forward to it as well. His gut told him this was the role that would propel her to stardom. He only hoped she was prepared for the ride.

When Jack turned, he noticed a guy in a suit, sitting with his laptop open on the table. The man glanced up and then back down dismissively.

That had been him not too long ago: independent, solitary, lonely.

If it weren't for Cece that would be him still. She had

loved him even when he was acting like a jerk. She'd fought for him—for them. For their happiness and for their son.

He glanced over his shoulder to see she, too, had noticed the man with the laptop. Rounding the table, she slipped her hand into Jack's. "You see what I mean?"

"Yes."

As they left the restaurant patio, her shoulder brushed against his arm and she gave him a playful bump. "I told you they had the best chocolate doughnuts."

* * * * *

Wonder what's going on in the lives of
Devlin Hudson and his new fiancée, Valerie Shelton?
Find out in this exclusive *short story*
by USA TODAY *bestselling author Maureen Child.*
And be sure to look for another story
in next month's HUDSONS OF BEVERLY HILLS,
TRANSFORMED INTO THE FRENCHMAN'S MISTRESS.

One

"Pick out anything you like." Devlin Hudson swept one hand in a wide arc to encompass the inside of the jewelry store. He glanced first at the woman standing by his side, then shifted a quick look at his gold wristwatch. He didn't have much time, so he wanted to accomplish this piece of shopping and get back to his already-too-busy day.

"Anything?" Valerie Shelton's violet eyes locked on his.

"Absolutely. And, if you can't find something you like, we'll try somewhere else tomorrow."

"I don't think that will be an issue," she countered, looking away from him to take in the exclusive shop stretching out in front of them.

Devlin had to agree. Cabot's was the finest jeweler anywhere. Practically an institution in Beverly Hills, Cabot's collection of rare diamonds and precious gems was world renowned. Which was exactly why he'd brought his new fiancée here.

"And you want me to pick out my ring myself."

"Seems easiest that way," Devlin told her. "That way you get just what you want."

Besides, he remembered a scene from a movie a few years before that had captured the imaginations of women everywhere. The hero had taken the heroine to Tiffany's and told her to choose whatever she wanted. And since Devlin was the COO of Hudson Pictures, where better to take advice than from a movie?

Still, Valerie didn't look pleased.

She nodded, but her expression was carefully blank. "I see."

Frowning, Devlin said, "I assumed you would prefer to choose your own ring."

"Oh," she assured him, sliding a look around the store again, "it's fine."

Still frowning, Devlin checked his watch again.

"Are we in a hurry?" she asked.

"I've got a meeting at the studio in an hour."

"An hour?" She stiffened, but that was probably just in his imagination since a moment later she said, "Then we'd better get started."

The soft sighs of harps and violins piped into the rarified atmosphere of the store through tiny speakers hidden behind trailing ferns. Several salespeople stood behind the glass cases waiting on customers and the owner, Henry Cabot himself, was hurrying toward Devlin. Not surprising, since over the years, Dev had spent a small fortune in this place on gifts for whatever woman he happened to be with at the time.

But those days were over. He was getting married and he wasn't the kind of man to cheat on his wife, even if he wasn't in love with her. Once his word was given, he wouldn't break it.

"I don't know where to begin," Valerie admitted quietly, and Devlin felt an inner sense of admiration.

If he'd brought any other woman to this store and given

them carte blanche, they would have been sprinting toward the gleaming display cases lined with sparkling gems. But Valerie was different.

His gaze raked approvingly over her trim, understated blue suit jacket and pencil-slim skirt. She wore a simple platinum chain at her neck and hammered platinum buttons on her ears. Her soft brown hair was pulled away from her face into an intricate braid and her violet eyes looked both pleased and cautious. She was everything he wanted in a wife. Elegant, well connected—being the only daughter of a powerful newspaper mogul—and quiet enough that she wouldn't be demanding too much of his time.

"Mr. Hudson," the owner said as he bustled up to meet them. "It's a pleasure to see you again."

"Thanks, Henry." Turning to Valerie, he added, "This is my fiancée, Valerie Shelton. We've come to find her a ring. Any suggestions?"

Henry's wide face lit up and his eyes practically danced. "Indeed, if you'll follow me, Ms. Shelton, I'm sure Cabot's will have the perfect ring for you."

"Thank you, Mr. Cabot. I'm sure you will."

Devlin walked behind her, admiring the sway of her hips and the slide of her tanned, trim calves as she walked confidently in a pair of sky-high blue heels.

Something inside him stirred and Devlin considered the attraction he felt for her a big plus. He wasn't interested in love, but lust was something else again. Lust was honest—blunt. Love was a trap for the unwary and that would never be Devlin Hudson. But being married to a woman he desired was essential. He wasn't a damn monk, after all.

Val's scent, a subtle blend of something both flowery and spicy, drifted in her wake and Dev felt that hard, hot something inside him fist even tighter.

As Henry Cabot drew out tray after tray of sparkling diamonds and sapphires, Devlin stood behind Val and told himself again that he was doing the right thing. It was time to marry, and Val was exactly the kind of wife a man in his position should have. Did it really matter that the rest of his family didn't agree? That they thought she was too shy, too quiet for him? He scowled briefly, then shook the thought away. He knew exactly what he was doing. He was insuring his success and the future of Hudson Pictures.

With his marriage he would seal a connection to the Shelton newspaper dynasty.

"What do you think, Devlin?" Valerie held up her left hand, to show him a ring. A huge, square-cut sapphire sat directly between two square-cut diamonds. In the overhead lights, the stones shone and winked at him as if they had a life of their own. He had to admire not only her taste, but the speed with which she could make a decision. Any other woman would have insisted on trying on everything in the store and he'd never make his meeting. But before he could tell her he thought the ring was a fine choice, his cell phone rang.

"One minute." Digging it out of his jacket pocket, he snapped it open. "Yes? No, you tell Franklin that he's not getting any more money for that stunt. He can CG it in post. Damned if he needs to build a spaceship for a fade-away shot, I don't care if he thinks he's an artist. That's what we've got special effects for." Frowning, Dev nodded at Valerie and held up one finger, to let her know this wouldn't take long.

Valerie shifted her gaze from her brand-new fiancée to the ring on her finger. It was beautiful, but suddenly it felt cold and heavy on her hand. And she wondered if she was making a mistake in marrying Devlin.

She knew he didn't love her.

Oh, he was considerate and attentive, but he was always

careful not to mention the L word, which, she supposed, was at least honest.

The problem was, she was in love with him.

She hadn't seen it coming. Hadn't really expected to fall for him. After all, she'd known from the first that Dev had only been dating her to get in good with her father. The Shelton newspaper group was a powerful force in the media. It wasn't the first time someone had paid attention to her to get to her father. But from the first, Val had been drawn to Devlin despite knowing all of that.

It had almost felt as though she'd been waiting for him her whole life. One look into Dev's blue eyes and Valerie knew he was the one for her. Yes, he was the same kind of workaholic type her father was, and she'd always vowed to steer clear of powerful men. But she'd seen Devlin make a real effort to spend time with her. He was always kind, thoughtful. And his kisses had quickened fires inside her she hadn't known existed.

Almost before she knew it, she'd been in love and it had been too late to back away.

"Ms. Shelton?"

"Yes." She forced a smile for the jeweler waiting for her decision. Behind her, Devlin was still talking to someone at the studio. "It's a beautiful piece, Mr. Cabot."

"Have you decided then?" Devlin ended his call and dropped into one of the fussy little chairs beside her.

She slid a glance at him. "Problem solved?"

"No," he muttered, tucking his phone back into his pocket. "Dealing with directors and producers, the problems are never solved. This one at least is postponed, though."

"Can I help?" She asked the question even knowing the answer.

"No, I'll handle it when I get back."

"Of course." Warning bells sounded in her head, but Valerie ignored them. She didn't want to be warned off. She wanted Devlin Hudson. But more, she wanted him to want *her*. It would just take time, she told herself firmly. She'd be the kind of wife he needed. She'd be there to listen, to help him, to offer suggestions. And one day, she thought, he'd wake up and find himself in love with her. He'd realize just as she had, that they were meant to be together.

There was a distance in him that tore at her. Val knew that beneath the surface of this carefully controlled man, there was a warm heart just waiting to be set free. She was convinced that she was the one woman who could reach him—change him—making him see that there was more to life than work.

"So," he said, nodding at the ring glittering brightly on her finger, "is that the one?"

"Yes," she said. "I love it. Thank you."

He gave her a smile that made her heartbeat stagger. Heat poured through her, settled at her core and she shifted uneasily on her chair. She wanted him and was almost nervous about it. Ridiculous, but then, it was ridiculous in this day and age to be a twenty-eight-year-old virgin, too.

Which was exactly why she had no intention of telling Devlin that he would be her first. She'd wait until after they'd made love for the first time—on their wedding night, as they'd both agreed to wait—and then she'd confess that she'd never been with anyone else.

"I should be the one thanking you," he was saying. "After all, you're the one who agreed to marry me."

"Well," she said as Mr. Cabot hurried off to write up their purchase, "then you're very welcome, Mr. Hudson."

Devlin leaned in, bracing his elbows on his thighs. Reaching for her hands, he took them in his and rubbed his thumb across the top of her new ring. "You won't be sorry, Val," he said. "I think we'll do very well together."

His touch sent more heat darting around crazily inside her and it was all she could do to keep her voice steady when she said firmly, "I think so, too, Dev. We're going to make a wonderful team. I know it."

"Is that for me?" Trey asked.

Cardin Worth cocked her head to the side and considered how much better the day already seemed. "Good morning to you, too."

When she didn't hold out the second cup of coffee for him to take, he came closer. She sipped from her heavy white mug, hiding her grin and her giddy rush of nerves behind it.

But when he stopped in front of her, she made the mistake of lowering her gaze from his face to the exposed strip of his chest. It was either give him his cup of coffee or bury her nose against him and breathe in. She remembered so clearly how he smelled. How he tasted.

She gave him his coffee.

After taking a quick gulp, he smiled and said, "Good morning, Cardin. I hope the floor wasn't too hard for you."

The hardness of the floor hadn't been the problem. She

shook her head. "Are you kidding? I slept like a baby, swaddled in my sleeping bag."

"In my sleeping bag, you mean."

If he wanted to get technical, yeah. "Thanks for the loaner. It made sleeping on the floor almost bearable." As had the warmth of his spooned body, she thought, then quickly changed the subject. "I saw you have a loaf of bread and some eggs. Would you like me to cook breakfast?"

He lowered his coffee mug slowly, his gaze as warm as the sun on her shoulders, as the ceramic heating her hands. "I didn't bring you out here to wait on me."

"You didn't bring me out here at all. I volunteered to come."

"To help me get ready for the race. Not to serve me."

"It's just breakfast, Trey. And coffee." Even if last night it had been more. Even if the way he was looking at her made her want to climb back into that sleeping bag. "I work much better when my stomach's not growling. I thought it might be the same for you."

"It is, but I'll cook. You made the coffee."

"That's because I can't work at all without caffeine."

"If I'd known that, I would've put on a pot as soon as I got up."

"What time *did* you get up?" Judging by the sun's position, she swore it couldn't be any later than seven now. And, yeah, they'd agreed to start working at six.

"Maybe four?" he guessed, giving her a lazy smile.

"But it was almost two…" She let the sentence dangle, finishing the thought privately. She was quite sure he knew exactly what time they'd finally fallen asleep after he'd made love to her.

The question facing her now was where did this relationship—if you could even call it *that*—go from here?

* * * * *

*Cardin and Trey are about to find out that
great sex is only the beginning....
Don't miss the fireworks!
Get ready for
A LONG, HARD RIDE
by Alison Kent.
Available March 2009,
wherever Blaze books are sold.*

HARLEQUIN® Romance®

This February the Harlequin® Romance series
will feature six Diamond Brides stories featuring
diamond proposals and gorgeous grooms.

Share your dream wedding proposal and you could WIN!

The most romantic entry will win a diamond
necklace and will inspire a proposal in one of
our upcoming Diamond Grooms books in 2010.

In 100 words or less, tell us the most romantic
way that you dream of being proposed to.

For more information, and to enter
the Diamond Brides Proposal contest, please visit
www.DiamondBridesProposal.com

Or mail your entry to us at:

IN THE U.S.: 3010 Walden Ave., P.O. Box 9069, Buffalo, NY 14269-9069
IN CANADA: 225 Duncan Mill Road, Don Mills, ON M3B 3K9

REQUEST YOUR FREE BOOKS!

2 FREE NOVELS
PLUS 2
FREE GIFTS!

Silhouette®

Desire®

Passionate, Powerful, Provocative!

SDES08R

You're invited to join our Tell Harlequin Reader Panel!

By joining our new reader panel you will:

- Receive Harlequin® books—they are FREE and yours to keep with no obligation to purchase anything!
- Participate in fun online surveys
- Exchange opinions and ideas with women just like you
- Have a say in our new book ideas and help us publish the best in women's fiction

In addition, you will have a chance to win great prizes and receive special gifts! See Web site for details. Some conditions apply. Space is limited.

To join, visit us at

www.TellHarlequin.com.

COMING NEXT MONTH

Available March 10, 2009

#1927 THE MORETTI HEIR—Katherine Garbera
Man of the Month
The one woman who can break his family's curse proposes a contract: she'll have his baby, but love must *not* be part of the bargain.

#1928 TALL, DARK…WESTMORELAND!—
Brenda Jackson
The Westmorelands
Surprised when he discovers his secret lover's true identity, this Westmoreland will stop at nothing to get her back into his bed!

#1929 TRANSFORMED INTO THE FRENCHMAN'S MISTRESS—Barbara Dunlop
The Hudsons of Beverly Hills
She needs a favor, and he's determined to use that to his advantage. He'll give her what she wants *if* she agrees to his request and stays under his roof.

#1930 SECRET BABY, PUBLIC AFFAIR—Yvonne Lindsay
Rogue Diamonds
Their affair was front-page news, yet her pregnancy was still top secret. When he's called home to Tuscany and demands she join him, will passion turn to love?

#1931 IN THE ARGENTINE'S BED—Jennifer Lewis
The Hardcastle Progeny
He'll give her his DNA in exchange for a night in his bed. But even the simplest plans can lead to the biggest surprises.…

#1932 FRIDAY NIGHT MISTRESS—Jan Colley
Publicly they were fierce enemies, yet in private, their steamy affair was all that he craved. Could their relationship evolve into something beyond their Friday night trysts?

SDCNMBPA0209